About the Author

June Oldham lives in Ilkley, Yorkshire, and spends her days writing in an attic from which she can see the moor. Between books she has held writing residences, and she does workshops and readings. As well as her books for teenagers and children, she writes novels for adults, one of which, *Flames* (Virago), was awarded a prize. Her leisure interests are theatre, film, walking, and conversation.

June Oldham.

Undercurrents

June Oldham

Hodder
Children's
Books

a division of Hodder Headline plc

A Catalogue record for this book is available from the British Library

ISBN 0 340 65147 4

Typeset by Avon Dataset Ltd, Bidford-on-Avon, B50 4JH

Printed and bound in Great Britain by
Mackays of Chatham, Chatham, Kent

Hodder Children's Books
a division of Hodder Headline plc
338 Euston Road
London NW1 3BH

To Patricia Ann Eyre, my sister

One

It was late afternoon. Heat hung over the ground, a presence you could touch. The trees bent, despondent, their colours faded; grass, once high and green-moist, stretched dry and flat like scythed hay. Cows followed the moving shade and settled under hedges. Over the fields and across the shrinking water the only sound was the click and scrape of a chain as a dog rose to pace briefly before returning to the shadow of the house.

In the room that had once been the parlour, a woman lay in bed and listened to the dog's noise. She raised her head and watched the sweat trickle down from the hollow of her neck and under her nightgown. With a crooked finger she pursued the drips as they slid between her breasts and flicked them out clumsily. Peering at her watch, she told herself, 'They'll not be long. Martin said he'd be meeting the coach at half past four. Should be near Crashing Beck Lane by now,' and she closed her eyes, picturing the road.

'That's Crashing Beck Lane,' Martin Helliwell told his passengers.

Dutifully Fergal and his mother stared through the

window of the car but saw only an overgrown path leading into trees.

'It runs down to the reservoir, what's left of it.'

'See there?' His wife pointed to a metal post on which was screwed a slim display box. Round its base the grass had disappeared, worn into dust. 'That's the bus stop for Niddford.'

Martin said, 'I expect you'd be happier biking it, Fergal. You're welcome to mine.'

'Thanks,' Fergal murmured while Madge Collins added, 'That's very kind.'

'You mustn't hesitate to help yourself to anything you need. You won't be putting us out, will they, Sonia? Not in ole Tennessee!' He slapped his thigh and attempted to yodel, making his wife laugh.

Tennessee! Fergal was envious. He wished he were going; it could only be better than here. For the last three miles there had been no other vehicle and it was at least ten minutes since he had seen anything recognisably a house. Barns, yes, he admitted, so perhaps they all crammed into them, along with the cows and sheep. He was beginning to wonder whether the country was one of those things that were fine as an idea but less satisfactory in practice. A possibility he had ignored when he had said to his mother, 'I'll go with you.' He heard her gasp, charmed, as a rabbit leaped across their path and bobbed into the hedgerow. Fergal glared at its pert scut.

The car turned off the road and stopped in a gateway. Martin nodded towards a tin box fixed to the wall, 'The postman delivers to here. We come and collect. The farm's no more than ten, twelve minutes' walk off.'

Pleased to relieve his cramped legs, Fergal got out and dragged the gate open. Beyond it, a track lifted over humped meadows and dipped into trees, its destination invisible. But as the car passed on to the track, its tyres crunching the stone chips and its engine picking up, there came the distant clamour of a dog's joyous bark.

The woman who lay in bed did not call to the dog to stop its noise. She waited, listened to the approach of the car, heard the engine slow down, the tyres leave the stones of the track and bounce over grass, then, through the dog's wild welcome and the clattering chain, the clang of car doors. 'Now, now, Gyp,' she heard her son call. 'Have you off that chain in a minute. Looked after her right, have you?'

Steps thumped down the path, reached the front door. A key scraped in the lock and the passage echoed as people walked down to the kitchen behind the woman's room. She listened, knew by the swift patter of heels that Sonia was leading, heard quieter steps that followed, then after a pause the squeak of rubber on the slate flags. These shoes halted, returned to the door, then began to climb the stairs, their owner burdened with cases. Her son directed, 'First on the left, Fergal,' and the shoes crossed the floor above her, a weight was dropped on the bed and its old springs twanged. 'The wardrobe and chest of drawers are empty. Just make yourself at home. We've put your mother on the opposite side of the landing,' her son explained. The voice that answered was a little hoarse, a light tenor, then it dipped suddenly to new depths and the woman exclaimed aloud, 'When she asked if she could bring her son, I didn't reckon on one grown!'

Flustered, she tried to tidy the counterpane, pull the sheet up to her neck, and ordered Martin as he entered, 'Set it to rights!'

'They aren't visitors, Mother,' he reproached her. 'Mrs Collins is in charge now.'

'No, I'm in charge. She's nursing.'

He shrugged, tired. 'Well, I expect it'll work out; you'll be kept comfy.'

She nodded, refusing to repeat what she had told him many times: that he and Sonia should not feel responsible for her, that they owed themselves a holiday.

'I'll fetch her. She's wanting to meet you. And her lad. He's a well set up young chap. Be able to help out if need be.'

'You needn't bring him in.'

'Why's that?'

'Tomorrow's soon enough. If I know lads, he'll not be that eager.' But her hand made an involuntary tell-tale pluck at the sheet.

Understanding, he soothed, 'I expect he'll have seen a nightie before now, Mother.'

'I shouldn't wonder. But tomorrow Mrs Collins can get me dressed a bit.'

'Sonia hadn't time this morning, you know that, what with the packing and having to go to the shops. There's nothing wrong with being seen in your nightie.'

A rebuke was sharp on her tongue, but she suppressed

it and answered softly, 'It may be silly, Martin, only I'll keep the pride. It's about all I've got left.'

Upstairs, unaware that he had been so decidedly excluded, Fergal heaved his suitcase to the floor and stretched out on his bed. He could hear his mother talking in the room below him; by the tone, level and monotonous, he knew she had put on her nurse's voice. That would soon pass, he hoped; it was to disguise nervousness. She had used it the day she had said: 'Have a look at this advertisement. Elaine's cut it out of the Nursing Times. I'm thinking of trying for it. Though it's years since I was nursing.'

He had assumed this was merely one of her sudden fancies, discarded as soon as the glamour wore off or, as his father would say, 'reality broke in.' Therefore he was unprepared when, weeks later, she told him, 'I've got that job. The patient's a rheumatoid arthritis case. Her son and daughter-in-law are going on holiday for most of August, so she needs someone to take care of her.'

'But why? Why are you doing it, Mother?'

'Well, one can always find uses for some extra money, but mainly I need a change.'

'Most people go on holiday when they want a change, not take a job.'

'That's what your father said. He'll manage perfectly well, of course. In fact, he'll hardly notice, he's away from home so often.' Her lips were pinched for a moment. 'And I know you can manage, Fergal. Do you mind?'

'No.' Feeding himself and his father for a month was a

small matter compared with the one that kept him awake. 'The job sounds like hard work.'

'The nursing won't be so bad; the techniques will soon come back. You don't forget them.' Then she added, almost to herself, 'I wonder what Mrs Helliwell weighs.'

What did his mother weigh? Eight stone?

She was saying, 'It's the rest of what has to be done that'll be hard. The farm's very isolated and I suspect there aren't any mod. cons. I might have asked Lorna if she'd like to come along, but she's got work experience in Coventry after she's done Intermediate.'

'I don't mind going with you.' He said it on the sort of impulse that he usually attributed to her, and she looked at him astonished.

'You? That's nice of you, Fergal, but you can't mean it. It wouldn't be much fun.'

It couldn't be worse than what he had to think about. It even might get rid of the thoughts, now and again. 'No hassle,' he told her. 'I could lend you a hand. Even two, if you wanted.' He spread them out. 'They're big enough?'

'Well, truly, Fergal, that would be marvellous. A relief. I admit I've been a bit worried. Not about the work so much as being on a farm – well, it's not a proper farm now, it used to be – miles from anywhere, alone except for an invalid woman. As far as you're concerned, I think it would do you good.' Now that her own anxieties were lessened, Madge was keen to find benefits for her son. 'In my opinion you've been working too hard recently. GCSE isn't for another year but it seems weeks since you went out and it's pulling you down.' Then she had repeated, 'A month in the country would do you good.'

'Set me up, would it? Bring colour to the wasting cheeks? That settles it, then.'

He had thought: I wish it *was* school work that was 'pulling' me down and he had gone up to his bedroom, thrust a CD into his stereo, screwed the knob to top volume and let the noise blast through his head. But it had made scarcely a dint on the memories.

Now, lying on his bed in this unfamiliar room, Fergal willed the memories away and forced himself to substitute more neutral events: leaving home that morning; the journey by train and coach; the meeting with Martin Helliwell; the halt to collect Sonia burdened with holiday shopping; the drive across moors, then high above a deep wooded valley – 'The river's down there,' Martin Helliwell had said; the abrupt turn on to a minor road and the glint of water through the weathered balustrade of a bridge; the entrance to the track which led to the farm; the rusting tin for the post; himself getting out to open the gate. And, recalling how he had heaved it off the latch, for it hung askew on its one sound hinge, he had caught a glimpse of white wedged between stones of the wall. Engaged with the gate, he had hardly looked at it. But now, his eyes closed, he examined it and saw a leaf of paper creased into two. Resting in the fold was a sprig of green.

His mother called, 'Fergal, supper's on the table.'

Below him, he heard the old woman's voice and her son's answer; wheels were trundled across the floor; china rattled.

7

That paper was probably someone's private postal service, Fergal said to himself. Or it could be the sort of note his mother put out: a request to the window cleaner, a reminder to the dustman, an order for extra milk. Amused by the idea of such messages left so far from the nearest habitation, he elaborated: Cows, Keep Off The Grass; Beware — Leaping Rabbits; Sheep — No Wool Today, Thank You.'

After supper he would walk to the gate and have a look at that piece of paper. Something to do.

It was an hour before the meal was finished and Martin and Sonia had said their goodbyes. On the point of leaving, Sonia looked tearful.

'You go and enjoy your holiday. You've absolutely nothing to worry about. I'm certain your mother and I will get on,' Madge Collins assured them, then added as extra comfort, 'And if we need any help, there's Fergal.'

'I can shift anything,' he told them. 'Specialities are Dutch dressers, treble size wardrobes, grand pianos and ten tonne trucks.' In fact, a boon to every invalid woman. As yet, however, he had not met this one; she was saving him up till tomorrow.

He gave them five minutes before following the car down the track. The heat had not diminished and by the time he reached the gate, he was sticky with sweat. When he pushed a hand into the crevice and withdrew the fold of paper, it stuck to his palm. However, it was not for that reason, but rather from a sudden inexplicable delicacy that he wiped his fingers on his denims before lifting up the little stem. It was a pale brown, almost hidden by green smaller sprigs that branched from it; in their turn they were circled by soft spikes of leaves. He saw on their undersides the silvery line down the spines and as he groomed the stem between his fingers he smelt its fragrance, sweet and fresh.

He did not know the plant or bush that the stem came from; he had never seen anything like it before. Carefully he replaced it in the crisp sheath and returned it to its place. Wondering what person had put it there, and why.

Two

Fergal was woken the next morning by his mother at his bedroom door. The smell of bacon and eggs gushed past her and into the room. 'It's going to be another scorching day,' she greeted him. 'Did you have a good sleep?'

He yawned in answer. His dreams, more suffocating than the temperature, were not to be shared.

'I didn't do badly, considering this is a new place,' she chatted. 'Once or twice I thought I heard noises but I dropped off again without bothering. Too tired. I've mentioned them to Mrs Helliwell and she said, "country creatures roam abroad, nights," which I suppose is natural. You'll have to go in and introduce yourself as soon as you've had breakfast.'

Mrs Helliwell had finished eating when he went into her room. In spite of the heat, she was wearing a knitted jacket which covered her arms and was buttoned to her throat. As she sat, pillows supporting her against the bed head, she had an air of waiting. He thought: She must do a lot of that. Unbidden, he removed the tray that was balanced on her lap.

'I'm Fergal Collins,' he told her.

'I was hoping you were. Otherwise I'd be asking for

explanations. As a rule I don't have a young lad striding in here offering a service. Or should I say, young man?'

He felt the blush on his cheeks. Only half an hour earlier he had examined them, as he did every morning, for the first hint of bristle. 'I'm not as old as I look.'

'That makes two of us, then.' Her eyes held his, challenging him not to fix her in a category, persuading him to understand it was pain, not great age, that etched the lines and greyed her gaunt face. 'There's not a lot of occupation here for one such as you. Different to what you'd have found once. Still, I suppose your mother'll get you jobs.'

He nodded; they were already listed. This morning's were to collect the post and look for the nearest shop. 'There's shopping,' he told her. 'Mr Helliwell said there's a grocer in the village somewhere.'

'Desmond Singleton. It's a tidy step.'

'I was wondering about a bike. Mr Helliwell said he has one I can borrow.'

She puffed out her lips, amused. 'Did he claim to have a cycle? *Martin*? Well, it's no lie, in itself, only he was tasking truth if he suggested he used it. It's the car all the time for him. He's as bad as any town man, the way he neglects his legs. You're not that kind, though, are you? You were out last night. Where were you off to?'

Annoyed at being asked to report his movements, he answered, short, 'Just down the track.'

'It wasn't an idle question; I thought there might be news.' She paused as if by chance he could supply it, then sighing, concluded, 'But all in good time. Now you'd better take the pots; your mother'll be wanting them to wash.'

He loaded them on to the dinner wagon and eased it over the mat by the bed, manoeuvring it round an ugly chair with a hinged seat he took to be a commode. At the door, he asked, 'So is it all right if I borrow the bicycle?'

'By all means. If you can't find it in one of the outhouses, it'll be in the top barn.'

'Where's that?'

'The quickest way's through the plantation at the back, but first time I'd advise you to go round it.' When she had given directions, she told him, 'There used to be a little foot-bridge over the gill but no doubt you can jump it, legs that length. I'm told the water's low.'

'It's been a hot summer. Still is.'

'Yes. Dries up the land.' As Fergal pushed the wagon into the passage, he thought he heard her murmur, 'Dries it down to the very bones, what's left of them. What they let stay.'

In the kitchen Madge was emptying a kettle of steaming water into the sink. 'There's no hot water tap,' she told him. 'Isn't that incredible? We use that.' She pointed to a large rectangular cylinder, its white metal surface cream with age. At the bottom of it was a tap. 'You have to fill it up and plug in. Thank goodness there's electricity.'

'It must hold twenty gallons.'

'This is worse than I'd feared. I'm not bothered about the outside loo but what do I do about the clothes? And the bed linen? Surely they don't wash it all by hand?' The prospect was intimidating.

'There's probably a machine in one of the outhouses. I'll have a look.'

'And what about baths?'

'If there's nothing in the bathroom for heating water, I'll carry it in buckets.'

'What a business.' But her grumble was less resentful. 'It's a great help to have someone to talk it over with, Fergal.'

He was relieved that she didn't say anything like: 'I can count on you,' or 'you're so dependable.' He attracted that kind of comment. On his school reports he was usually summed up as: Overall, a good, steady worker and a reliable member of the class. He wished people could find other descriptions for him, descriptions that made him sound rather less boring. He would love to shake them all up, find something to do that shocked them. But nothing ever came along. He was stuck with his temperament, born with it. People seemed to lean on him, came to him when they were in a mess or wanted some help. He could hardly say, 'I don't want to know, mate. Get lost!' Dependable Fergal.

But even that was not true any longer.

It wasn't true, but not for a lawless, exotic, sparkling reason. Not for a reason he could treasure, hug to himself and say, 'I've proved I can be more exciting. I did *that*.' He wasn't steady and reliable any more, not because of something he had done but because of something he had failed to do. He couldn't be depended on, and the joke was that only two people knew it. One was Bailey.

Fergal stretched to the draining board and picked up a washed glass. Fiercely he screwed the tea towel into it and listened to the low squeak. The other person who knew, of course, was himself. And that was worse.

'I've no idea how long it would take you,' his mother completed an explanation. He had a sense that it had gone on some time.

'Sorry?'

'Are you telling me you haven't been listening? Really, Fergal, I do wish you wouldn't switch off. I was talking about you going into the village. Sonia told me that it's three miles by road but there's a path somewhere.' She made a gesture which took in the whole of the land round them.

'I'm going to look for the bike.' He had let himself in for living in a primitive farm house, drying up, lugging water around and shopping, but he wasn't committed to tramping over fields when he could cycle down a perfectly good road.

At the back of the farm was a yard surrounded by cowhouses and stables; beyond them was a plantation of firs. It rose steadily above the house and was bounded by a wall. Fergal strode by the side of it until he came to its end and the fence Mrs Helliwell had mentioned. After that, her directions were out of date because he could see no path but, taking a diagonal route up the meadow, he came to a narrow gully. Down it a gill trickled weakly without spray or splash, and crossing it, he did not wet his boots. On the other side, he entered a spinney and

15

through the trees he could see the barn.

He could not imagine what its original purpose had been, so far from the house, but it had degenerated into a handy dump for farm litter. Standing at the door, Fergal contemplated the flattened tins of tractor oil and the thick plastic bags that had held sheep licks, fertiliser, cattle cake. There was a heap of straw in one corner and in front of it a sad, rust-eaten bicycle.

It was stupid to expect anything else, he told himself. She said Martin stuck to his car. Why should he want a bike? He might as well chuck this thing in here, along with the rest of the rubbish.

Fergal stood the machine on the handlebars and seat and examined it. Something inside the pedals clicked warningly; the brake pads were loose; rust so pitted the wheels that they threatened to break into perforations. However, they turned quite smoothly when they were spun. Encouraged, he thought: Perhaps I could do something with it.

As the wheels slowed down and came to rest, he saw, at the junction of a spoke and a rim, a nut of soil. It was clay coloured, dense; a small remnant of mud. Idly he flicked at it then, since it remained stubbornly attached, he put a thumb nail under it and levered it away. Though dry on its outer surface, he found that underneath, where it had been wedged to the metal, it was damp. He examined it, intrigued. Someone had used this bicycle, this clapped out wreck, recently, definitely this morning, and had ridden through wet mud. Where, in this weather, in this baked country, had anyone found that?

It made him hesitate to take the cycle. Someone had ridden it, and that seemed to assert ownership.

On the other hand, it belonged to the Helliwells and they had said he could borrow it. So he would. Quickly he swung the cycle on its wheels again and dragged it out of the barn.

'So this is the bike!' his mother said, meeting him in the yard. 'Was it really necessary to carry it?'

In his thoughts he replied: You try pushing it along that path! A lot of his talk to his mother never entered her ears. He lowered the cycle from his chest and rubbed his groin where a pedal had ground in.

'You'll give yourself a bad strain one of these days.'

That was a routine remark and did not merit even a silent answer.

He propped the cycle against the house wall. Gyp sniffed round it, whining dismally.

'You've worried her, Fergal, bringing that in. It should have been dumped.'

'It'll be OK. It only needs oiling, cleaning up.' He explained because although she was a nurse, she was not very practical. Perhaps she had lost the habit. Anyway, she was dim about machines. He watched her run her fingers along the handlebars as if checking for dust, then squeeze the brake lever. She warned, 'These brakes should be tightened.'

That only showed how she could surprise you at times.

The rest of the day and the next Fergal spent servicing the bicycle. In the stable, now empty of horses and car, he found oil and lathered it liberally but there were no tools.

The tyres were flat but he couldn't pump them up, nor, if they were punctured, could he remove the inner tubes without levers. When he appealed to Mrs Helliwell, all she could suggest was: 'They're no doubt somewhere in the house, and the pump. Martin never left that on the bike. He considered the pump would be the first thing that would take the fancy of a light-fingered gentleman.' Her tone mocked her son's choice of securing the pump rather than the cycle, but Martin's peculiar logic seemed to have been inherited. In explaining that the front door could be locked but it was customary to leave the back door open, Mrs Helliwell had said, 'The back's for those without a key.'

'Somewhere in the house' offered a wide scope for a search. 'All I want is a few simple tools and a cycle pump,' he complained to his mother as he rummaged through drawers and cupboards in the kitchen, looked into the case clock and the oven at the side of the huge range.

'I should try the dairy,' she advised.

The door to this was at the far end of the kitchen and gave on to a flight of steep steps. Burrowed into the slope of the land, its stone walls white-washed and its floor paved with slate, the chamber was cool, almost chill, a refreshment after the heat. Round the walls, at working height, was a deep shelf cold to the touch. On it, the milk had been cooled in bowls, the cream had waited for the churning and the butter had been made into pats. Now it was a repository for jumble ranging from yellowing newspapers and empty mineral bottles to dented saucepans, gas cylinders and a whole squad of Wellington boots. Scattered among these were cardboard boxes crammed with tools. There was one for every conceivable job, but most showed little use; many of the tools had not been removed from their plastic display packets; others partially assembled lacked crucial parts. In one box were tins of paint, most of them unopened. The collection would have delighted a DIY medallist, but after the rush to equip himself, this person had given up. Equally neglected were tools of a more ancient vintage, all pocked with rust. At last discovering a bicycle pump, Fergal was anxious in case it would not work, but a stream of air squirted out of it when he pumped. There was also a little tin containing a kit for repairing punctures. With these finds, plus spanners and a pair of pliers, Fergal was armed for his task.

He was pleased to have it. Adjusting the brakes, cleaning the chain, he had plenty to distract him. He could chat to Gyp while he scoured wheel rims and handle bar until only the pits made by rust speckled the bright steel. As he scrubbed the seat and polished the spokes his eyes were kept away from painful visions. When he removed a wheel, levered off the tyre, blew up the inner tube and plunged it into a bucket of water, the bubbles he saw were miniscule and did not break accusingly against his ears. The tube was firm, it did not flop as it was lifted out of the bucket. It was not limp and sodden. When it was pressed, it did not cough up water. All it needed was a patch.

Three

By the time Fergal had the cycle ready, there was a sizable shopping list waiting. Madge suggested he ask Mrs Helliwell if she had anything to add.

'No, there's nothing I want from the village.' She stressed the last word. 'But you might do something else for me.'

'Yes?'

She drew breath to answer, then let it sigh out. Hooked fingers dragged across the sheet until they were caught in a fold. 'It'll keep,' she murmured. 'I can wait.'

'I shan't be long.'

'That's a fact, on that bike.'

He had taken it into her when she had demanded, 'Let's see what you've been up to,' and embarrassed, he had listened to her compliments and exclamations of surprise. 'You've made a good job of that. I could have done with you here eighteen years back; you might have thought it worth going round with a paint brush and knocking in a few nails.'

He recalled the unused tools in the dairy but he did not feel he could ask her to explain.

'Why don't you take Gyp?' his mother asked as he left.

21

Understanding, the dog leaped and fawned.

'I was going to.'

'Don't forget the post.'

Because he knew she was hoping for a letter from his father, he told her, 'If it looks urgent, I'll bring it straight back before going on to the village.'

With a bicycle you were mobile and careless of time. Later he would explore; he could go miles; he might find something more interesting than this run-down farm and its meadows of thirsty grass.

He pushed back the door of the stable and strode to the place where the cycle waited. After the dazzling light of the yard it was a few moments before his eyes could adjust, but they only confirmed what he already suspected. The bicycle was not there.

Incredulous, Fergal looked round, as if it might have wheeled itself to hide in a corner or, sprouting wings, it had flown up to the rafters to roost. Then he left the stable and hunted through the sheds and outhouses, arguing to himself that his mother might have moved it. Finally he had to accept that the cycle had gone.

Fury boiled through him. He shouted at Gyp, 'What were you doing to let someone pinch it? Are you supposed to be a guard dog, or what?' Seeing the dog's tail droop and her head lower, he relented. In any case, perhaps Gyp knew the thief, so had not prevented him. Fergal remembered the back door was always open. For 'those without a key.'

Someone must have seen him working on the cycle. Someone must have discovered where it was, and watched. I'm being paranoid, he told himself; no one passes here; the farm's at the end of the track. Round him, the country was silent, empty. But behind the house the rising ground provided vantage points for observation; the plantation afforded good cover and the cycle had not been taken until it was ready for use. Fergal looked at his hands still traced with oil and groaned. He'd been a pushover, a sucker, somebody's dupe.

He did not go into the house and report that he had no cycle; he did not wish to listen to sympathy. Instead, he wanted to put the whole thing behind him: the farm, this stupid holiday, the wasted labour. So leaving the yard accompanied by Gyp, he strode fast down the track.

The 'tidy step' that Mrs Helliwell called it took Fergal over an hour. Though he kept up a good pace, he knew only the general direction and he was frustrated by lanes which ended with a gate and a notice warning against trespassers on Water Board property. Eventually he found the road that led to the village; it had one long street of plain houses and a post office and grocer combined.

Few people were about, but in one of the gardens a woman knelt by a herbaceous border hunting for weeds; a man was adjusting an aerial on a roof; another was driving his tractor into a farm yard. As Fergal passed them, they nodded or murmured 'Good day' and when he entered the shop the owner held his hand out for the list with the words: 'Better let me have that. Simpler. I know Mrs Helliwell's preferences.' Answering Fergal's surprise, he explained, 'Oh, we could see where you'd come from. We all know Gyp. I've got one of her pups.'

When he had packed the groceries into bags, he said, 'After you've carried these back, you'll have earned a holiday. There's plenty to see and the Dales Show's on middle of the month. You should go to that.'

Fergal thought: I would if Bailey were here. His mother had said, 'Perhaps Mrs Helliwell wouldn't object if Bailey came for a few days. We can pay his keep.' But he had shaken his head and gone out to avoid questions.

'The Show's only four, five miles off. An easy walk if you go top end of the reservoir,' Desmond Singleton told him. Then, hesitant, 'You'll have had a stroll round?'

He did not like to admit that he had not seen it, did not even know where the reservoir was. 'I haven't had time yet.'

'That I can believe! It seems you keep busy. I'm told the heat's drying it out, top end. Not something I'm anxious to look at, myself, but you'd have no trouble with it being a stranger.'

You're right I'll have no trouble with it, Fergal answered silently. I hope I'm not so desperate for something to do I have to go and gawp at a reservoir!

One thing he had already decided to do was return to the barn to see if there were clues to the person who had taken the cycle. It must be the same one, he argued, who had ridden it earlier. In a countryside so sparsely populated, it was unlikely that two people wandered near an isolated farm picking up a bicycle whenever they could lay hands on one. But he didn't visit the barn that day. After reaching the farm, his feet dragging, not from fatigue, he insisted to Madge, but from starvation, he enjoyed a lengthy lunch, then there were household chores.

'My arms have been nearly pulled out of their sockets carrying those bags,' he complained, 'and I don't see why I have to do this anyway. I don't at home.'

'We haven't a yard at home,' his mother pointed out, 'and this looks as if it hasn't been brushed up for months. Would you please stack those bin bags of rubbish in the shed while you're at it?'

'You mean, while I'm brushing up? Are you asking me to brush up or stack bags? I can't do two jobs at once.'

'You would if you were a woman; you'd do half a dozen.'

'Then why don't you?'

However, his objections were only token; he did what she asked. She had taken on an exhausting job and hadn't he said he would give her a hand? Strictly speaking, he hadn't been offering to brush up yards or act as a dustman but he'd rather do that than what she had to do, help Mrs Helliwell to the commode or dry the skewed fingers, their knuckles gross and crammed. He did not know how to deal with them. If he avoided looking, she would know he thought them repulsive; if he looked, she might conclude he was getting a perverted kick out of things so monstrously abnormal. When she kept them under the sheet, he was discomforted by the suspicion that she guessed his dilemma.

She had them hidden when she called him to her. 'Have you got a minute?'

He indicated the brush and risked a joke: 'Not many.'

Her smile made her look younger. 'I can hear you toiling and your mother's just told me you had to go on Shanks's pony to the shop. It seems the bike's got a customer. It was a better bet after you'd finished with it.'

Usually if anything were stolen, the owner was distressed and outraged but her answer did not surprise him. He was learning that things here were different.

He told her, 'I wouldn't have bothered if I'd thought it might be nicked.'

'Nicked? Ah: made free with. Don't take on about it. There must have been the need and who are we to measure that?' Her eyes left his and turned to the window. 'As things are, it'll be a brave soul that goes abroad.'

He wanted to demand: What are you talking about? What do you mean, brave soul, and *as things are*?

She was still looking out of the window, but he realised that she could see little of the country beyond. A trellis for a climbing plant had loosened and lolled across the panes, and a few yards away a laburnum hung cascading pods, obscuring her view.

'I might be able to fix that trellis. Was that what you wanted me to do when you asked this morning?'

Roused, she considered his question. 'No, it wasn't that. I was wondering whether you'd mind taking a look. Or have you seen?'

It was assumed he would know the place she referred to and he remembered the shopkeeper's asking: 'You'll have had a stroll round?' He could not understand their interest in a stretch of water, an artificial lake. 'I suppose you mean the reservoir. Where is it?'

'Where is it?' she echoed. 'But why should you know? It's there.' She pointed through the window. 'Front of the house, in the valley — what was a valley till they flooded it.'

To make a reservoir.

'I'm told it's going down, Fergal, and if it's sinking past Church Bridge . . .' She could not continue. It had been an effort to speak the last words.

'I can easily go and have a look.' Only a few hours earlier he had resolved not to bother.

'Would you? It's top end I'm thinking of. Yet, perhaps,' she hesitated, seeming to withdraw her request, but she frowned at herself and told him, 'Best way's through the woods; they're a step or two up the track.' She pointed again through the window. 'There's a path turns off it.'

Once begun, her description was precise, minutely detailed: an oak smothered in ivy; a stile with the bottom rung broken; the exposed roots of a beech under which rabbits had burrowed. Her tone became confident, warm; Fergal sensed that she was seeing the path as it had been when she was a girl, and the places where she and her friends had played. And he thought of Bailey and their times together: copying homework; pooling pocket money; yelling encouragement to football heroes; giggling over magazines; choking on their first and final cigarette.

Following her directions that evening, he discovered that the path had not altered; its landmarks remained. The only difference was the gills. On Mrs Helliwell's advice he had borrowed Wellington boots from the dairy, but he did not need them. The clefts in the hillside were not filled with rushing water but were thin runnels and he wondered whether, in the two days since he had crossed it, the gill near the barn had dried up. But Crashing Beck, the fifth stream Mrs Helliwell had named, was wider and though grass had invaded its edges, its flow was not broken by the stones on its bed. Here he turned and walked with it, downwards, until it fell through rusted sluices; there were tumbled walls, suggesting a mill. Below him, the beck drained between steep banks, then these lowered and vanished under a long, flat expanse, chrome bright, mirroring the sky. The reservoir.

Fergal jumped down the mill's collapsed walls and made towards it. Keeping to the side of the beck, he was in a narrow strip bordered by trees; it widened and his boots lifted dust. The earth was bare, uncovered by grass or shrub. Fergal halted. As Crashing Gill curved and merged with the reservoir it spread round an arching parapet – the span of a bridge. On each side of it were rectangles of dressed stone which occasionally rose to several courses round the base of a chimney; inside were hearths. He was looking at the remains of houses that before this drought had been submerged.

He did not go any further. The place made him uneasy. Once it must have been like the village he had visited that morning. Now it was silent, dead. He felt as if he had trespassed upon something that he had no business to see.

Affected by these feelings, he was not eager to meet Mrs Helliwell when he returned to the farmhouse and she seemed in no hurry to hear his report. She did not call to him when he walked down the passage or send a request after his mother had prepared her for the night. When finally he took her supper, she did not interrogate him, merely remarked, 'This heat's gone on so long, I'm beginning to dry up.'

'You have to take plenty of fluids.'

'Yes, that's what's needed.' Her face lowered; she scratched at a biscuit, scattering crumbs. 'Else everything'll be sweated off. Nothing to see but skin and bones.'

He guessed that she was talking in symbols and he was annoyed that she could not ask him outright. He said, 'I think there'll have to be a lot more sun before it gets down to that.'

'I don't like the idea of anything left not decently shrouded.'

'Some's showing, but the beck hasn't given up.'

Her hand, the terrible stiff claw, trembled; she looked up and he saw the apprehension on her face. So he told her, hearing his voice gentle, 'I can see the top of a bridge.'

'Thank you, Fergal.' And she whispered, 'Please God let that be all.'

Four

The water they used at the farmhouse came from a spring. There was a pump in the yard but its spout was rusty, its handle making a prop for the gate. Nowadays the water was drawn from a pump in the kitchen. This fed a tank and stood in a corner, about waist high and boxed in, with a lever projecting from a long slit at the top. If you didn't press the comparison too far, you could pretend that the lever was the handle on the bar of a pub and as Fergal worked it backwards and forwards he counted the number of pints he had pulled. He had no idea how much water entered the tank per pull but he hoped it was two pints and doubled his total when he had pumped for thirty minutes. Done every morning and tea time, it was a boring job but, giving the lever a powerful tug, he told himself that soon he would be in prize winning form.

He was glad that someone had gone to the expense of having water piped from the spring. Then he had stopped before installing a way of heating it, though he had put a bath in a scullery. Perhaps the money had run out, or the person had lost interest. Like buying all those tools in the dairy. Tasks were half completed, or never begun.

This was consistent with the house, with its general

appearance of neglect, with the fact that the land was no longer farmed. He remembered Mrs Helliwell's: 'I could have done with you a time back.' It was as if something had happened, a line had been drawn and after that they had given up.

Fergal swore to himself. He hated being a prey to such fancies but they were difficult to shrug off. He wished he were at home messing about on the computer, going to the match. Here all he could find to do was to stroll up to the barn.

Having taken his previous route round the wall that bordered the plantation, he climbed the fence into the meadow. Four days before he had made a faint stripe of paler colour in the grass where its stalks had bent under his boots; today he thought he could make out a deeper bruising and convinced himself that these were the impressions of wheels.

But reaching the barn, he found no cycle. Disappointed, feeling foolish for such optimism, he turned to go, but the place was not quite as it had been. It looked tidier. There were still the empty tins and plastic bags but he could not recall that they had been heaped together; nor, as far as he could remember, had the pile of straw been arranged as if to make a bed. He walked over to it and lay down. This isn't a bad place, he thought, if you want to be hidden.

He did not know how long he remained there. He had dozed off and was roused by points of stalks scratching his arm. Turning over, he disturbed the straw, and a fragrance rose out of it, sweet, fresh, associated with silence and dusk. Sniffing, he followed the scent and found, wedged between the straw and the wall, a slim roll of fabric. Inside lay stems of a plant.

There was no need for him to examine them. He had looked closely at a sprig like these five nights earlier, but he inhaled deeply, appreciating their fragrance, before he folded them again in the fabric and put the little parcel in its place. Then he stirred the straw where his body had flattened it and checked that he left no prints or scrape of a boot in the barn's dust. When he was back at the farm he searched through the garden, urged by a hunch that the plant would be there, and he found it, a healthy bush, its leaves moist and bright beside the faded spent flowers. He nipped off a shoot and took it to his mother.

'What's this?' he asked her.

'Rosemary. Where did you find it?'

'In the garden.'

'I thought everything in it was dead! Is there much?'

'A good bit.' Silently he added: But there won't be for long. Because he had seen where stalks had been cut and expected that more would be taken.

'I didn't know you were interested in herbs, Fergal.'

He shrugged but could not resist saying, 'I am now.'

He was asking himself: Why should anyone steal rosemary from the garden, hoard it in a derelict barn, stick a piece of it in a dry stone wall? Some loony? Some kleptomaniac grabbing herbs that are no use to him? Probably took it the same night as he had stolen the bike. Fergal corrected: No, not the same night, because the rosemary had been cut before that; the piece in the wall was there before the cycle had been taken; and that had not been done on a whim to possess a thing bright and desirable, a jackdaw theft. Not until it was completely repaired had it been reclaimed.

He thought of the mud on the wheel and wondered whether it could have come from near the reservoir. That seemed to interest everybody he met. During the afternoon, a farmer arrived with his tractor and trailer to collect the rubbish and stated, 'You'll have been down to it,' then interrogated Fergal on day, time, and visible details. Like Mrs Helliwell and Desmond Singleton, he did not seem particularly bothered that the water was retreating, more about what it was leaving behind.

They're all bunged up with country superstitions, he reasoned to himself. Mrs Helliwell had said: I don't like the idea of anything left not decently shrouded.

These words, mingled with more personal memories, lurked at the edge of dreams and made his night restless. At last, to banish them, he forced his eyes open as he had taught himself in the last weeks. He had discovered that sleep often returned unharassingly after a wakeful pause. The trick was to prevent his mind touching painful or difficult subjects. So he threw back the sheet, recited a list of formulae and then hummed his favourite track. Halting, he became aware of the quiet, but it was not the one he had made. It was the silence of listening. He could feel it as precisely as he could see his jeans on the chair, his bed lit by the last paring of moon. Then as no more sounds came from him, the silence withdrew and Fergal thought he could distinguish murmurs that alternated in tone, made by two speakers. They rose from the room below.

For a moment he thought: Mrs Helliwell needed attention; but there had been no call to his mother. Uncertain whether he ought to investigate, he waited, heard the latch on the door click and along the passage a few muted, slow steps.

He hesitated no longer, slid off his bed, looked round for a weapon, found nothing more fearsome than his camera, and held it against a leg. Throughout the house the curtains were not drawn and, guided by moonlight, he crept from his bedroom and down the stairs. He had no plan of what to do when he came upon the intruder; he assumed that he would find him in the parlour, a neat dapper figure rifling the drawers for loot. He had not expected that it would be empty and untouched. Nor in the passage was he prepared for Gyp lying drowsy and peaceful outside Mrs Helliwell's room. And when he stood on the steps that led into the dairy, he was surprised to see, propped against the wall, not a rifle but a long stick; its handle was of antler, fashioned from a tine.

He walked back through the kitchen. Across the passage, a slit of light showed under Mrs Helliwell's door. He had to open it, but he feared what he might see. In spite of its absence elsewhere, it was blood that his imagination gave him as he knocked. Hearing her answer, he felt his body relax.

'So you're wandering,' she greeted him.

'I heard voices. Noises.'

'You were making a few noises yourself. Reciting something or other.'

'I woke up and I was trying to get back to sleep.'

'We all have our ways, but you won't manage it standing there.'

He couldn't believe they were having this conversation after someone had walked into the house, talked with her, sneaked into the dairy. Why the dairy? Looking for something? he wondered.

'I thought there was a burglar.'

Mrs Helliwell's lips twitched. 'And what were you going to do? Take a photograph?'

He looked down at the camera and felt ridiculous. 'I hadn't anything else.'

'You've got a stick.'

'I found it in the dairy.'

'Then I'd be glad if you'd take it back. That's where junk's kept in this house.'

But it hadn't been there when he'd searched for tools and he had seen that she recognised it.

Exasperated, he thought: She's playing games with me. So he told her, 'I'll keep it upstairs, just in case.'

'You'll do no such thing.' Her voice had risen. 'You put it back exactly where it was. Do you hear me?'

His alarm of the last five minutes was changed to anger and his stare told her that if he chose he could drop the stick and walk out. 'I heard, and another time a whole cartload of tramps can come into the house if they like and knife us all in our beds. It's not my responsibility.'

Immediately he was ashamed of his rudeness, embarrassed by the wild ludicrous words, but she nodded as if she did not consider his outburst unreasonable. 'That's how it is,' she answered.

Trying to recover and suggest sense and maturity, he told her, 'I'll put the stick back, then, but I'd better lock the door before I go up.'

'I'd rather you didn't, Fergal.' Her tone was low now, almost pleading. 'You can think I'm exaggerating, like you, but if ever the day comes when that door is barred against any creature, I'll be put in my box.'

It was not until he was lying in bed again and going over their talk that he realised the final remark was Mrs Helliwell's concession that someone had visited her, and even then it had been sidelong, oblique.

Next morning, Madge said, 'Do you know, Fergal, there was a dirty cup on the draining board when I came down. I don't remember leaving it. I could swear I'd washed everything up.'

He had disturbed their night visitor before he had had time to remove evidence. So Fergal did it for him, saying, 'I had a cup of tea, Mother, after you were in bed,' because he had decided not to tell her what had happened. It was definitely something Mrs Helliwell preferred to keep to herself, and though he was mystified and irritated by her behaviour, he thought he should honour her wishes. This worried him. It meant he was putting the old woman first and deceiving his mother, but he argued that Madge would be happier not knowing. She had pretended to admire the convention of the unlocked door, exclaiming, 'Isn't it marvellous? Such a change from where we live!' However, if she learnt that someone had, in fact, taken advantage of it, she would lie awake all night listening for noises.

She said to him, 'I hope you haven't anything important planned for today. I want you to help me with the washing.'

Visions of himself armpit deep in suds replaced the scrambled eggs on his plate.

Interpreting his expression, she reassured him, 'There's a launderette in Niddford.'

'I can't get the stuff there! I haven't even got a bike.'

'Give me credit for some sense, Fergal. I'm not asking you to heave suitcases of linen down the track and wait for a bus. There's a man, a Mr Beardsall, who has a petrol pump somewhere.' She waved vaguely through the window. 'And he has a sort of taxi service. I've booked him mid-morning. If you came, you could look after the clothes while I do some shopping; there are lots of things we can't buy in the village.' She smiled, anticipating pleasures.

'I don't imagine Niddford will be stuffed with shopping malls or department stores or the usual High Street branches,' he cautioned.

'No, of course not. They'll be more homely.' Already absorbed in the prospect, she reached for a pencil and pad.

Fergal sighed. If there was one thing he thought he would never understand about women it was their fascination with shops. He was pleased to discover that Mrs Helliwell was an exception.

'I'm told you're off to Niddford,' she observed, as he collected her tray. 'Shopping.'

'That's Mum. I have to watch over the clothes in the launderette.'

'Another guarding job?' It was her only reference to the events of the previous night. 'Well, I reckon you've got the best of the bargain. It's one benefit being like this; I've said goodbye to shops.'

He nodded. Two humps under the coverlet indicated the swollen, clenched feet.

'I remember my grandmother saying, she was growing deaf, "I have to count my blessings; I don't hear every bit of twaddle coming out of folks' mouths." And that's twaddle, too, I expect, as far as you're concerned.'

'I don't mind.'

She had not mentioned her condition before or referred to anything in her past and he sensed that it was her way of apologising for her secrecy over her visitor. So he heard himself add, 'I do quite a bit of remembering myself.'

'Doubtless, and it's not borne easy by the look of you sometimes.'

He did not answer and, searching his face, she said no more.

'Is there anything you want from Niddford?' he asked.

'No, thank you; but there's an errand I'd like you to do if you will.'

'Yes?'

'It's to deliver a . . . package. There's a junk shop half way up the main street, well it used to be for junk but nowadays Crispin Farnley thinks: Give it a bit of a tarting up and I can call it antique. The man to see's named Walter Ibbotson.'

'Where is the package?'

'Upstairs. In a room in the attic, what used to be mine. There's a writing desk with a drawer under the top. You'll find it in there. You can't mistake it; there's nothing else.'

'Is there a message?'

'Only tell Walter I sent it. He'll know who it's for.'

At the end of the landing on the first floor was a narrow arch hung with a soft chenille curtain. Once Fergal had pushed it aside and seen the next flight of stairs but had not explored. Now he discovered two rooms, their ceilings sharply pitched. One was full of lumber which he did not stop to examine; the other was furnished and, though dusty, the glass in its skylight smudged with the droppings of birds, it was not scruffy or shabby like the rest of the house. Glancing round, he saw the lace shawl on the sofa, the rug pastel-coloured and sheened like velvet, the shelves of mahogany filled with leather-bound books. Almost every inch of wall was covered by water-colours, all landscapes. They bore little interest; he merely noticed that the same initials were on them all. He stepped towards the skylight. Beneath it was a dainty escritoire. Lying in its drawer, as Mrs Helliwell had described, was the package. A lump of sealing wax with a thumb print's whorl had been pressed over the wrapping's edge. Staring up at him, written in ink round the wax, were the words: Black Monday. Fergal winced with distaste.

Lifting out the package, he heard the clink of metal as the contents shifted and, his fingers pressing, he felt three slim cylinders. Down the longest one there was definitely a line of raised disks and there were a number of others, he thought, on the shorter cylinder. He turned the package over and found, near the end of the middle size one, a hole. Not cylinders, he said to himself: tubes, and intended to fit one into the other. Thus he deduced what the package contained. He had not learnt to play one, but he had messed around with instruments in the orchestra at school.

He went down to the kitchen, wrapped more paper round the package and put it in a plastic bag, asking himself what could be meant by Black Monday and why it was linked to a flute.

Five

Mr Beardsall's car was antiquated and of no recognisable make.

'What is it?' Fergal asked him, defeated.

'I call it Beardsall's cruiser. It was a wreck first off. But if you look round, you can soon find what's needed and after that it's only a matter of a blow lamp, welding and sweat. If you'd like to load up, I'll nip inside and pay my respects to the old lady.'

They had two suitcases crammed with bed linen and clothes. Fergal heaved them into the boot but he kept the plastic bag. As he settled in the passenger seat, his mother asked, 'What've you got in there, Fergal?'

'Something Mrs Helliwell has asked me to deliver – I can while the clothes are in the machine. She didn't say what it is.' Mr Beardsall was fiddling with a wing mirror, listening. 'But I can tell you what it feels like: three sticks of gelignite.'

Behind him, Madge laughed and swung her legs on to the seat, but Gilbert Beardsall's face stiffened and his fingers tightened round the mirror. 'We had a bellyful of that, gelignite, a time back.'

The rest of the journey passed in silence.

Inside the car there was no remission from the heat. It converted the roof into a solar furnace and, since Mr Beardsall's passion for welding had not stopped at the windows, they were almost impossible to wind down. All that Fergal could achieve was a small slit; it sucked in a cooling draught but his body soon warmed it up. He would have removed his T-shirt if the previous occupant had not been a depilating dog; he didn't wish to be stuck with its hairs.

In his side mirror he could see the wheels of the car raising a thin wake of dust; it lay gritty on the windscreen, streaked the bonnet, filming its colour with drab, and it sprinkled the hedges by the side of the road. Above them, the leaves of the trees looked pinched, their colour hinting at autumn. The whole countryside was exhausted, begging for rain. Fergal wondered how much more of the submerged village was rising out of the drying mud.

When they reached Niddford, Mr Beardsall said, 'I've to go to Skipton now, there's a little job I have to do, and pick up a battery. I could be back here by two thirty, if that's agreeable, Mrs Collins.'

'Yes. I've left some sandwiches and drink with Mrs Helliwell. We can have a snack lunch.' Her eyes were searching the street, hungry for shops. Fergal thought: It's pathetic, her being so eager, like a kid expecting a treat. She must be as fed up as I am, living in such an isolated place.

The town was small; most of the shops were tucked into lanes leading off the main street. When Fergal finally tracked down the launderette, he found that he was the only customer. He filled two machines, followed the instructions concerning detergent and coins, and went in search of the junk shop. It was distinguished, as Mrs Helliwell had predicted, by a sign 'Antiques', but the display in the window could quite happily have assimilated the farmhouse lumber. Inside the door, its mount dingy and speckled, was a small water-colour and he paused to look at it.

'A lot of people are fascinated by that,' Crispin Farnley commented brightly in the hope that this time fascination would lead to a sale. 'Of course, it has a rather special interest at the moment.'

Fergal tried to look non-committal. 'I should like to speak to Mr Ibbotson,' he said.

'Ah, Walter. He's in the workshop. I'll call him,' the other offered, resigned to the loss of a customer.

Walter was a stooped man in an apron mottled by wood stainer. It had dyed his fingers and mapped the lines on his palms. He showed them, saying, 'You'll excuse me,' as Fergal introduced himself. 'Martin Helliwell told me the arrangement there was for him and Sonia to go away. How do your mother and you find it, then?'

'Not bad.' What else could he say? Miserable, tedious, lonely? 'I suppose it has its moments.'

'That's likely. Up there.' Like everyone Fergal met, Walter gave his plain words a significance. 'And Mrs Helliwell?'

'She seems fine. She asked me to give you this.'

Walter took the plastic bag but he did not look inside

it, merely folded the top over and tucked the roll under his arm.

'Mrs Helliwell said you'd know who it's for.'

'Yes.'

'That's that, then. I'll get back to the launderette.' But he hesitated, sensing that the man had something he wished to say. 'Have you a message for her?'

'No. I'd like to wish her health but . . . Anyway, it seems she's in good hands.' Then, carefully, 'You'll see to her, won't you? You'll know what I'm saying. You look an understanding sort of young man.' He turned away before Fergal could answer.

As he left the shop, he looked at the water-colour again. It showed a stone bridge over a brook; behind it were trees and the slender spire of a church. He scrutinised the initials in a bottom corner.

'Irresistible isn't it?' Crispin Farnley attempted persuasion. 'I concede that some people might consider the mount's rather on the dubious side and you might prefer to replace it. I'm ready to discuss a price allowing for that.'

'I'll think about it.' He couldn't imagine it up on his bedroom wall jostled by posters; but neither would he have imagined he could come across another picture done by A.G. who had painted others he had seen. Hanging in an attic room.

The launderette, though not exactly a hive of activity, he reported to himself, was noisier than before. Two more machines were in use, vibrating frenziedly, and somewhere in a store closet was the rattle of buckets and mops. Unheard except when these sounds dipped, water gushed into a sink. This stood in a recess by the driers and Fergal's first glance was perfunctory; then he looked back. Because someone was standing at the sink taking off a T-shirt and over the shoulders and tight across the back were the unmistakable straps of a bra. Fergal stared.

The girl took up a cake of soap and began a thorough wash, unhurried, methodical. She squeezed out a cloth, lathered it, then holding an end in each hand, she slung it over her head and slapped it diagonally to and fro across her shoulders. As it went down her back, he could see the skin was fine and unblemished, white where the T-shirt had been. She soaped her legs, rinsed them, dried herself with a frayed towel, then dunked the T-shirt vigorously. When she had wrung it out, she pushed the soap and cloths into a rucksack, pulled on another shirt, called, 'Bye, Tracie,' and turned. Seeing Fergal, she exclaimed, 'I didn't know you were there.'

'It doesn't matter.' His blush answered hers.

'Tracie doesn't mind. I asked her.'

'It's none of my business. Anyway, you didn't strip down.' He wasn't sure whether he was relieved or disappointed.

The girl laughed. 'I did think of that. The launderette's so quiet.' Then she laughed again because at that moment she had to raise her voice over the noise.

She walked forward and stood beside him. Seeing his face clearly, no longer against the light, she gasped, 'It's you!' Then, quickly, stumbling: 'I've seen you before,' and gestured towards the street.

'I didn't know I made such an impression.' It was the style of comment he would adopt for girls in his class, aiming to sound casual, urbane, but today he could not hit the right note. Because the girl was embarrassed by the reason she had given for recognising him. It sounded false.

'Before I came in,' she persisted and the blush flared again. Now he was certain she lied.

'I had to deliver a parcel. This stuff takes ages.' He was talking to camouflage his thoughts. 'A lot longer than yours.' He pointed to the T-shirt dangling from her hand.

'It'll soon dry.'

'Yes.'

'I'd better see to it.' But she did not move. She considered, her right hand stroking a cheek. At last she muttered, hoarse, 'I'm sorry, but I can't explain.'

He watched her stride to the door, asking himself: Why don't I follow her? Why don't I tell her: There's nothing to explain; you made a mistake, that's all, thinking you knew me when you don't; we're strangers; you didn't have to pretend you'd seen me in the street.

It was stupid to make such a fuss when there were so many other things they could have talked about. Such as why she washed herself in a launderette. Was she on holiday walking through the dales, sleeping rough? He could have asked her: Why don't we meet up? He had three more weeks to get through and they stretched flat and colourless, empty of company. He could have told her about Mrs Helliwell's visitor, about the flute.

The girl was not as tall as he was but older, probably in

the sixth form or a student. She looked strong and competent. As she walked away, he had seen that her thighs were deeply tanned below the shorts, her calves plumped by muscle and strangely rashed, not with spots but with tiny scratches and specks as if lightly punctured.

He was still thinking about her as he left the launderette and he envied her freedom from luggage. All hers comprised was a rucksack and he hoped she would not bump into him weighed down with the two cases. Wherever he went, they made him conspicuous and his mother aggravated this feeling; she was smothered in parcels and bags. Anyone else, he grumbled to himself, would have arranged to leave them and pick them up later, but she held on gleefully; they spelt the morning's success. She chatted non-stop, describing her adventures with the greengrocer: 'She'd run out of strawberries so she let me have some from her own garden;' the iron-monger: 'He sells nails by the pound, but I only wanted a scrubbing brush;' the butcher: 'The lamb was fattened in the meadow you could see from his window!' the baker: 'Everything made on the premises!' and there would have been the candlestick maker, too, Fergal groaned to himself, if they hadn't been out of business for centuries.

While all this was being reported, Fergal scrutinised the menus outside a café and two tea rooms and concluded dismally that anyone wanting serious food would have to set out and forage for it. Finally however, they found a public house that could provide something substantial and he ordered a hamburger and chips.

At last coming out of her ecstatic reminiscence, his

mother remarked, 'I'm making a proper meal this evening, Fergal. Will you be able to eat it if you have that now?'

He took particular satisfaction in answering, 'Yes.'

Lunch improved his spirits; he even agreed to look at a jersey his mother thought might suit his father and he could smile at Mr Beardsall's comment, 'My goodness! If I'd thought you were going to buy Niddford out, I'd have brought the truck.'

'I enjoyed that,' his mother announced unnecessarily as she climbed into the car, 'but I don't like leaving Mrs Helliwell. You could come any time, Fergal.'

Since there was a possibility he would see the girl again, he answered, 'I might.'

'Good. It would make a change from hanging about round the farm.'

'I don't get much chance to hang about!' He added silently: And in future I'll keep well out of the way when there's a job.

As they approached the track that led to the farmhouse, his mother said, 'I wonder if there's anything in the second post.'

'I'll look.'

There were two letters in the tin and a post card. Glancing along the wall, he saw that the little fold of paper was still in the crevice, a leaf of the rosemary poking out of the end. There was no reason why it should have gone, the only people who stopped at the gate were the postman and the man who delivered their milk, yet its remaining there bothered him slightly. It was like a sign others might interpret but which was unintelligible to him.

'There's a post card for Mrs Helliwell and this for you.'

Taking the letter, she saw it was from his father and for a moment it trembled in her hand, then it was slipped into her bag. She murmured, 'I'll read it when we get in.'

He could understand her desire for privacy; his own letter was in a pocket well out of sight.

As soon as they reached the farm, he went to Mrs Helliwell in order to replenish her carafe of water and hand her the card. She studied it with an exaggerated concentration that told Fergal there was to be no mention of Walter Ibbotson and the flute.

'It seems Martin and Sonia have arrived safely,' she summarised. 'He says they're having a lovely time. A pity he can't think of anything better to write. He can disappoint me, can my son. What'd you put on a post card?'

'I don't know.'

'Come, now!'

'Dear Martin, Just had a smashing morning at the launderette. Your bike's been stolen and we've got a walking stick in exchange.'

She smiled. 'I'll have that put on one to them, some of it. Now you make yourself scarce. It's your mother I need at the moment.'

After that, he did all that he could to delay opening his letter. He let Gyp off her chain and played with her in the plantation behind the house; he peeled the potatoes; he took his time pumping in the water; he helped clear the pots after supper; he watched an old Clint Eastwood film on television. But whatever he did, the handwriting on the envelope kept sliding across his vision until he could ignore it no longer and went up to his room.

The letter was short and in Bailey's usual style. He could turn out stunning essays, get his points across pithily and not bother with padding. Once his English teacher had commented: Lucid and well argued but some time you might try to relax your rigorous commitment to brevity.

Dear F, he wrote, *Yesterday outside the station Groper Trent shambled into me and asked, 'Is it true what Striker Morrison says, like Fergal's staying in a rave place with thousands of birds?' Of course I said, Yes, and left him dribbling lasciviously. How close is S.M. to the correct number?*

Also: Why such a moody sod at the end of term? It seems to date from the incident in the river. That's history now.

You could have a go at an answer, if you can spare the time. I've been thinking about all that frolicking in the hay that used to go on. Can you do it in silage? Yours, B.

Fergal folded the sheet of paper, then unfolded it and read again, 'the incident in the river. That's history now.'

But it wasn't. As far as he was concerned, history was stuff that was over and done with, and this stayed with him as if it had happened that very day.

Six

As soon as Fergal sat down to breakfast, his mother said, 'I've got two suitcases packed with wet clothes. Weren't there any driers at the launderette?'

'Yes. Sorry. I forgot.'

She tutted. 'You must have been dreaming.'

'That's right.' And what about? he imagined the next question, and wondered what she would say if he told her. 'Can't the stuff go outside? It'll be dry in minutes.'

'And be stiff as a board. I like them to have a good fresh blow.' She said this as if one could occur in a drier.

'I'll put them out,' he offered, to make amends.

A coil of rope hung in the dairy and there were hooks in the walls each side of the yard. One pulled out as he looped the rope over it. He considered making another hole but, having unearthed a drill, he could find no bits for masonry. An attempt at improvisation – hammering a nail into the mortar – failed, so he found a ladder, put it against the wall of the stable and, praying that it would hold, he attached the rope to the bracket that supported the guttering under the roof.

When he had pinned up the clothes, lifeless in the still

air, his mother told him, 'Fergal, I've come without any stamps.'

He knew what she was asking but said, 'I'm off on a walk. Taking Gyp.'

'Couldn't you go by the village?'

'Mother, you don't go *by* the village; you have to go *to* it. For three miles. You could've bought stamps yesterday.'

'I could, but yesterday I didn't imagine I'd need them.'

That closed the argument. He suspected that something was going on between his parents, so if Madge planned to answer his father's letter he'd no wish to hold out on the stamps.

'I'll get some.'

'Lovely. Phil hopes you're "enduring", and he sends his love.'

'Thanks, and I am, just about,' he reported back, appreciating his father's word.

The trek to the village did not seem as long as it had done the first time, either because he knew the way or, like an engine, his legs were run in; another of his father's expressions. When he reached the shop, Desmond Singleton was standing outside it giving directions to two walkers. 'You can't miss it,' he was assuring them. 'Second lane on the left past the hall, keep going to the cross roads, then turn left again and about one, two miles on, you're there.'

They thanked him, hitched up their day sacks and strode out, their great hiking boots clomping.

'It's raising some interest,' Desmond remarked,

automatically assuming that Fergal understood what 'it' was. 'I've directed them to the dam. None of us'll think they need to see anything else. I hear you've taken a look. Mrs Helliwell ask you?'

Fergal nodded.

This seemed to permit the man to talk more freely. 'I always said: What if there's a drought? They maintained there was no risk of the water dropping, plenty in the river, and they'd calculated the flow of the gills. Calculated! They couldn't tot up six items on a ready reckoner! First time they filled it, trial run, the church spire stuck out high as a telegraph pole. An accusing finger.'

'I didn't see that.'

'You won't. They soon got rid of it, after they'd let out the water, and set about what was left of the houses. Sent in the bulldozers and the rest of the demolition mob.'

'What was it called?'

The man hesitated, then he said, reluctant, as if the name were difficult to pronounce, 'Linden. They've struck it off the maps. Now it's only an area, as you might say, not a proper place. But it'll always be more than that to those they pushed out.' His voice hardened. Fergal saw his fingers clenched over the edge of the counter and was reminded of Gilbert Beardsall's grip round the wing mirror of his car.

Desmond continued, 'Do you know how long some people's families had lived there? Generations. Their names are there on the graves. And they thought – those that wanted the water – nobody'll object if we give them compensation. Compensation! Money! When they shovelled us out of our homes, out of our valley, like so much horse muck! And dumped us elsewhere. There's no compensation for that. They wouldn't listen to us telling them they could easy build the reservoir higher up the river and not trouble any creature save a few beasts and sheep.'

He halted. 'Well, that's enough of that. You didn't come here to listen to me holding forth.'

'It's all right,' Fergal muttered. The man's passion and bitterness made him uneasy.

'I wish I could say it was finished and done with, only the water's dropping and memories are long.'

'Yes.'

'So where will you be going now?' Desmond asked, calmer, when he had sold Fergal the stamps.

'I might walk to the dam.'

'It's an easy stroll. You'll find the water's deeper there. Linden's a way up stream; it's shallowest at that end.' He then ushered Fergal outside and with much pointing and snaking of hands, repeated the directions.

The road down to the dam was narrow but in good repair; it continued along the top of the massive structure and then ran up the valley before entering a cultivated wood. On one side of this bridge the water of the reservoir lapped against the great concrete wall. Fergal could not estimate how deep it was or how far the level had dropped, but despite the dried mud along the banks, the reservoir did not look puny. It remained a thing to be respected, hinting threats. Quickly he turned from it and crossed to the other side of the dam. Here water was conducted along a built channel and into a shallow stream. This was the continuation of the river that entered the reservoir 'top end', but which from this position could not be seen. Near the dam, neat vertical rocks were evidence of blasting. Fergal understood why on the previous day Gilbert Beardsall had not smiled at his joke about gelignite.

The hikers who had been in the shop were standing in the middle of the bridge, the woman looking at the reservoir through binoculars and the man scrutinising a map. He glanced up as Gyp ran to him, sniffed round his legs then sank on her belly, watchful. 'It's amazing how you can train them,' he remarked. 'I wonder if you would help us. We want to get to Linden.'

'It's not there any more. It was flooded when they built this reservoir.' He tried to imitate the local accent since they assumed he was from the neighbourhood.

'Yes, of course,' the man said, impatient, 'but the location's here.' He tapped the map.

'We understand that it's beginning to show up,' the woman explained.

'There are a few bits, but nothing that's worth seeing.'

'All the same we'd like to have a look.'

The man interrupted. 'The shopkeeper said we should start here, but there are no marked paths. Perhaps if we got to the edge of the reservoir we could walk round?'

'I don't advise that.' Desmond Singleton had told him: I've directed them to the dam; none of us'll think they need to see anything else. 'It's Water Board property and they keep putting notices up about danger,' he said, hoping to warn them off.

'What sort of danger?'

Good question, Fergal answered silently and improvised with: 'The land's been under water years now; it's not stable. I can tell you a better way if you're set on going, only it'll take longer.'

'That doesn't matter,' the man said, bold in his boots.

So Fergal put his finger on the map, traced it along the lane up the valley side, across minor roads, over moorlands, up hills and down sudden escarpments.

Watching them march over the bridge, he was astonished at what he had done. He ought to shout them back, tell them the huge detour was unnecessary, somehow talk his way out of his deceit. But he had found their curiosity offensive. Nobody wanted their prying, creeping round, pointing. Not Mrs Helliwell or Mr Singleton or Mr Beardsall or, in some way, Walter. And without Fergal's realising it, they had drawn him in.

He walked back to the end of the bridge and climbed the fence that bounded the reservoir. 'That's not saying I approve,' he told Gyp. 'It's not logical, being anxious about a few heaps of stones.'

Days later, remembering that comment, Fergal was to smile grimly at how inadequate it was.

Beyond the dam, woods on the sky line enclosed the reservoir and at the foot of the trees was a continuous shelf of coarse grass. Its roots were exposed, dangling, marking exactly the water's former height. Below this shelf the sloping ground was terraced by narrow stripes;

they were made by the descent of the water as sand is ridged by an outgoing tide. Along them a meagre grass sprouted, but walking by the verge of the water Fergal was in a desert of dried silt crazed with cracks. He found this sinister, as if he had been marooned on a barren planet, and he was glad of Gyp's company. When he came across the prints of tyres, for a moment they seemed to signal danger, some kind of threat.

There were two sets of them and they bordered the water, one was well over thirty centimetres away from it and the other no more than eight from the brink. Each set comprised a thin weaving line with another running straight through it, pressed by the back wheel. For they had been made by a bicycle and when the ground was still wet. Traces of mud would have remained on the tyres.

Fergal said to himself: That doesn't mean these tracks were left by the cycle I fetched from the Helliwell's barn.

Proof was impossible. The tread was so bald it left no pattern and if it had done, he would not have recognised it. Not like Sherlock Holmes. He grinned at the memory of Holmes once declaring that all makes of tyres had different treads and he could identify every one. Even so, you couldn't dismiss the coincidence: a cycle that had been ridden through wet ground, and not far away in a barn a lump of mud between the spokes of a wheel.

But looking more closely, Fergal discovered a clue that he could interpret. In the tracks that were further from the reservoir, the one made by the back wheel was broader than the other, whereas the prints close to the water were the same width.

'What do you make of that, Watson?' Sherlock Holmes would have demanded.

'There have been two people here, Holmes, for it is clear that there have been two cycles.'

'A plausible deduction but incorrect, my dear fellow. The tracks have been made by the same machine. Those further from the water were laid down when the back wheel was flat, and since those that are nearer show a more equal inflation, the cycle was used here again after young Fergal Collins had patched the inner tube belonging to the back wheel and blown it up.'

'Your powers of deduction are amazing, Holmes.'

'Yes, but this was a simple matter. Now we must next ask why any person should subject himself to the fatigue of riding round this rather undistinguished reservoir. And remember – not once, but twice.'

'I'm completely at a loss, Holmes.'

'So am I, Watson,' Fergal said aloud.

The cycle tracks continued along the edge of the water until, nearing Linden, they left the brittle scabbing silt and vanished into the dust.

Annoyed that his hunt had gone cold, Fergal halted and for the first time, because he had approached from the dam, he saw the river. It was separated from Linden by a thick promontory of land and, no longer flooded over, its banks clearly defined, it ran in a curve down the valley. Then it descended into the reservoir by abrupt rocky steps. Somewhere he knew that it must be joined under the motionless reservoir by Crashing Beck.

He turned towards this and walked between fallen

walls that had once bordered a lane. It took him up the bank into Linden. There the water had dropped so far that the whole of the church bridge could be seen, complete, undamaged, leading to a spread of dressed stones. It was not possible to distinguish which had once formed the nave or the spire.

As on the first occasion he had come, he did not linger. He did not enjoy contemplating the ruins of these houses and the knowledge that day by day more rose out of the reservoir's bed. Although the heat quivered above the bare soil and his shirt was soaked with sweat, he was suddenly cold. He felt as if he had entered a tomb.

'Gyp! Dinner,' he called; then, 'What is it?' Because the dog was splashing under the bridge, whining. Fergal slithered down the dusty bank and looked where the dog sniffed.

He knew immediately what it was but he would not let himself acknowledge it until he had drawn one of the stalks through his fingers and smelt its scent. Instead of a single stem, like the one that lay in a crevice of a wall, there was a substantial bunch. It hung from a twist of white ribbon that had been pushed between stones of the bridge's span, then secured with a plug of wood.

With Gyp at heel, he scrambled up the bank, strode by the beck and climbed through the ruins of the old mill. As he took Mrs Helliwell's path to the farmhouse, he wondered how soon someone would plunder the herbs in its garden to replenish the store in the barn; but it did not require the masterly analysis of Sherlock Holmes for him to be sure that it would be the same person who had removed the bicycle, who had ridden it in the mud fringing the reservoir and had placed that wreath of rosemary under the church bridge.

Nor would the faithful Watson, however overawed by his friend, have hesitated about the fact of a figure hurrying through the trees. Before reaching the farm house, Fergal saw it several times but it did not come near enough for him to make out any details except that it was quite tall.

In the kitchen, he said, 'Do you mind asking Dad if he would send Grandfather Collins's binoculars, Mum?'

'I thought something had happened to you. Look at the time. Aren't you hungry?'

'Starving.'

'You could always pack some sandwiches if you intended to roam around.'

'I might do that. Will you ask Dad?'

'I don't know when I'm going to have time to write. Why don't you drop him a card?'

'O.K. No hassle.'

A faint tinkling came from Mrs Helliwell's room. Madge explained, 'I found a little bell in the dairy. What a mess that is! It's nicer for Agnes to rattle a bell than having to shout. Do you mind seeing what she wants while I make a pot of tea?'

'I hope it's not much,' he said gracelessly, his hunger aggravated by the sight of a dish of salad and cold meats.

Mrs Helliwell was wearing a knitted bed jacket but she hooked it up to her chin as he entered. 'Ah, Fergal. I recognised your step. I was hoping it'd be you.' She paused, looked round as if searching for a reason for her summons. 'There's the window.' It had two panes moved by sashes that were threaded inside the frame. 'Could you open it a shade more?'

Fergal pulled, but the window refused to be lowered further. 'I'll have to look for a hammer and a chisel.'

'They should be somewhere.'

'Do you mind if I wait till after dinner?'

'Not at all.' But she had not finished; she was not letting him go; she was waiting, her breath in wisps, her eyes pinched against the thing he had to tell her.

'I've been to the shop,' he began.

'It took you a while.'

'Afterwards, I went to the dam.'

She nodded, impatient.

'Then I walked along the reservoir to Linden.'

She flinched at the name. A crook of a finger scratched at her throat.

'You can see all the church bridge. Not just the parapet.' He felt like a torturer.

'It'll not go back now.'

'Not till we've had months of rain. There were two people at the dam wanting to look but I pointed them the wrong way.'

She smiled approval.

Then he said, 'And there's something else.' Immediately he regretted the impulse to tell her. 'It doesn't matter.'

But she forced him with: 'What is it?'

'Under Church bridge there's a sort of spray. Someone

63

has stuck it there. It's made of rosemary.'

'Rosemary! Are you sure?'

'I've seen some in the garden. Mum told me what it is.'

'Rosemary. It's for remembrance.' Her head swivelled on the pillow and she whispered, 'For remembrance. What creature living would not want to forget?'

Fergal turned away, silently repeating her last words.

Seven

Fergal stood in the attic lumber room. It housed the overflow from the dairy, tools and equipment that had belonged to a farrier or smith: tongs, irons, horse shoes, tangled harness, and great horse-collars whose leather was stained pitch colour and seams were split. Amongst these were two draped sheets. Under the first was an easel; the second concealed a wheel chair.

His mother had remarked, 'I don't know why – I imagine it's the heat – but Mrs Helliwell's been rather low these last three or four days.' This was since she had heard about the rosemary, but Fergal thought it was wiser not to complicate his mother's diagnosis. 'I'm wondering whether we could give her a change of scenery. Martin sometimes carries her into the kitchen and I've suggested we do, but she didn't like the idea. I suspect she feels it's not dignified, relying on a boy. There's a wheel chair in the attic, she tells me. I could get her into that.'

He managed to lift the chair and heave it over the junk. A wheel spun and a finger was trapped in the spokes. He cursed loudly. His mother, everybody, took a delight in giving him jobs designed for a fork lift truck. He wouldn't have them wished on him if he were small and weedy; at the moment he couldn't think of a single benefit in being his size. And, when it came to the crunch, there was no guarantee that being hefty would be any use. Fergal paused, his hands slackened their grip.

His muscles had failed him. Suddenly they had not been there any more. They had leaked through his skin like sweat; his arms had gone solid, his fingers would not grapple and all his feet would do was nudge at the water, an unyielding transparent syrup, while his breath gave out and the stuff flooded his mouth and lapped echoing round his skull.

The wheel was still spinning. He regarded it for a moment, not seeing, then carried the chair on to the landing. Shutting the door on the rest of the lumber, he thought of the easel and wondered how long it had stood there, out of service and covered by a sheet. Perhaps it had belonged to the same person who had painted the pictures in the other attic room. He would have another look at them.

This time, he examined the pictures closely. They were dainty, scrupulously detailed, views of houses, woodlands, rills, farms, lanes, avenues of trees. The style was modest, eschewing experiment; what was extraordinary was the repetition of subjects. It was as if the artist so loved them that he had been driven to paint them over and over again. One was a view of a church almost identical to the one hanging in Farnley's Antiques. However, there was a distinction: instead of the A.G. in the corner, the picture in the attic was signed A.G.H. Unquestionably all were the work of the same person but about a quarter bore the longer signature.

He stepped back, telling himself: You're a dim head not to have guessed. Mrs Helliwell's name is Agnes; the card from her son was addressed to Mrs Greaves Helliwell. Presumably Greaves was her maiden name and she had added the H to the paintings she did after her marriage. The reason he hadn't imagined that she might be the artist, he admitted to himself, ashamed, was that her hand was a helpless claw. When you looked at her, you couldn't imagine her being any different; you took what your eyes gave you without thought: she was just an old cripple. Like people assumed he was an adult man because he stood six feet.

The chair was almost the same width as the staircase from the attic, so he walked backwards, jerking the wheels down the steep rises to bump heavily on the narrow treads. The next flight was easier but there was an awkward turn and a loose cushion slid off the seat. With it was dislodged a thick folded paper. He pocketed it, threw the cushion to Madge and hoisted up the chair to clear the bannister rail.

'Be careful,' she called. 'Don't strain yourself.'

It's a bit late to think of that, he answered, sorry he couldn't waste breath to say it aloud.

At the bottom she told him, 'I don't know what I'd do without you.'

'You might soon find out.'

For some reason, she found this amusing. 'Well, just give me plenty of notice. I'm looking forward to settling Mrs Helliwell in this chair. An afternoon outside should do her good.'

Fergal decided he had had enough of domesticity. 'I'll take Gyp for a walk.'

Now having a clearer notion of the area, he calculated that by striking straight through the plantation behind the house he would come to the road that led to Niddford. That would be shorter than the route from the farm track. Not that he could get to Niddford without a cycle, but he might thumb a bus. Optimism'll be the death of you, he told himself wryly. He thought of the brisk sweep of a soapy cloth across naked shoulders. 'I can tell you,' he told Gyp, 'there are more interesting things to do in that town than haul laundry about and deliver flutes.'

After the raw sun it was cool under the trees, but Fergal was soon through them. They ended at a stone wall, a stile of flags set into it. From there a path led through fields until, as Fergal expected, it reached a lane. Gyp ran ahead, squeezed through a gap by the gate and immediately Fergal heard her snuffling whimpers and a woman's low voice.

She was sitting in the shadow of a hawthorn, a half-eaten apple in her hand, and she was wearing the T-shirt she had drubbed so vigorously in the launderette. Her face was more tanned than he remembered and her dark hair was polished a warm chestnut by the sun. When she turned and saw him, her spontaneous expression was welcoming, happy, unguarded.

For a moment he was so astounded that he should meet her again, a fact not fantasy, that all he could greet her with was a limp Hi.

'Hi!' she echoed. 'This is a friendly dog. What's he called?'

'She. Gyp.'

The girl fussed, her fingers combing through the thick coat. Gyp rested her snout on the girl's knee, luxuriating in the attention.

'I'm taking her for a walk.' It was useful to have a handy subject for conversation but he wished it weren't a dog.

'Better than taking the washing.'

He laughed with her. 'Do you go to Niddford often?' It sounded a bit like the 'do you come here often?' that he and Bailey parodied with: Do you come to this massage parlour often? To this sauna (mixed)? To this bordello? This loo?

She smiled as if guessing some joke. 'Just now and then. You had a load of washing.'

'Two, as a matter of fact.' Laundry was no better a topic than the dog. 'There aren't many modern conveniences where I'm staying. It's a farmhouse, the other side of that plantation.' He waved behind her.

'Is it all right there?'

'Not much going on.'

She plucked a blade of grass and wrapped it round a finger. 'Where you are must be Water Board property, so do you work for it?'

He would think about the Water Board property bit later. 'No, I don't work for it. Why do you ask?' The question was a way of stalling, trying to avoid the confession that he was at school and, not only that, but still a year short of the sixth form.

She shrugged, had lost interest. Then graceful,

uncurling her legs, rising, she told him, 'Time to get on.'

She was about to go and he had managed nothing. The irises of her eyes had amber flecks in them; he didn't even know her name. He had to delay her. Forgetting that she had to resort to washing herself publicly, and ignoring the rucksack she was lifting on to her back, he asked, 'Do you live here?' His voice was too loud.

The question stopped her hands righting the straps on her shoulders. 'Live *here*? No, I do *not*. It's the last place where I'd live. I wouldn't live anywhere near this lot. Not if they got down on their bended knees and begged.'

He was too shocked to speak but at last he muttered: 'Why's that?'

'Shall we take it that me and them . . . we simply wouldn't get on.'

Discomforted by his stare, she said, hinting apology, 'Well, there you are. That about wraps it up.'

Fergal nodded.

'Don't think I make a habit of shooting my mouth off. Only I happen to feel quite strongly on that particular subject.'

'Takes all sorts.'

She bent down, murmured, 'Bye, Gyp,' while she smoothed a thumb round the soft fringe of the dog's ear. Fergal found it hard to reconcile her harsh outburst with such gentleness. Rising, she pulled at the hem of her shorts and he saw again the pink rash of scratches on her legs.

'Well, best of luck.' She held herself straight, at ease with her height, mistress of herself. Except that she could not control a trembling along her lips as she waved farewell.

Fergal watched her walk down the lane, unable to sprint after her, to say: Look, can't I join you? If you're hiking in the Dales, perhaps you'd like to come back to the farmhouse, have supper. My mother's a fantastic cook. That wasn't a particularly irresistible invitation. There might be squash courts somewhere. Or ten pin bowling; she'd be good at that.

He ought to have said to her: Let's go into Niddford, there must be a bus some time. It doesn't matter to me what you think about this part of the world, I'm not all that fond of it myself. And I don't care if you hate everybody's guts. But he couldn't have said that. A week ago he could have done, but not now. Today, he could not have made it sound convincing.

He felt listless, as if they had had an argument, broken off their relationship (when they hadn't got one) and he didn't want to tire his mind out by going over it. What he most wanted was to lie in the shade of the wall and go to sleep.

When he returned to the farm Mrs Helliwell was sitting in the wheel chair contemplating the derelict garden. 'This was nice once,' she told him. 'But it's been let go to pot. And you don't look much better. Anybody'd think you'd lost a florin and found a tanner.'

'I'm alright.'

'I'm not saying I think you're sickening for anything. Except company. That can be a trouble round here, your age.'

Not inclined to discuss it, he asked, 'Shall I push you nearer the hedge?' The sun slanting between trees had found the chair.

'That would be kind. Your mother's been running out all afternoon, chasing after the shade. I hope it wasn't too much of a bother carting this monstrosity down from the attic.'

'No trouble; and I don't mind pushing you out, see if I can shift it over the fields.' He pointed to those in front of the farm. Divided by walls, they stretched into the distance hiding the drop of the land to the reservoir in the valley, the diminishing river and the drying becks. He told her, 'You'd be able to see more.'

'I can see all I want,' she answered sharply.

He thought: It's not my day. I only have to ask a simple question like: Do you live here? or offer to shove this one in an antique wreck across fields and I get strips torn off.

'You mustn't worry about it,' Mrs Helliwell said, softer, 'and it was you we'd got our minds on. You should take a walk to the next village; there's a public house there but you'll not get served anything you're not entitled too. Richard Allerton's severe.'

'I don't know anybody.'

'You soon would. They're friendly enough, and there's the off-comed 'uns, too, this time of year, shaking down in the old cottages they've done up. That's apart from the day trippers or those on the hoof passing through.'

'I haven't seen many.'

She acknowledged his smile and told him quietly, 'But I reckon there's one you like.'

Startled, he felt his cheeks flush.

That evening as he pumped up the water Fergal reflected on Mrs Helliwell's last comment. There could be no doubt that it referred to the girl. It was yet another piece of information that the old woman had. How did she get it all? The telephone was not in her room but she had visitors. Gilbert Beardsall had gone inside to 'pay my respects to the old lady'. So had the farmer who had collected the rubbish. And how often do people come in the night? he wondered.

Thinking of this, he continued to pump until he felt his mother behind him.

'Stop a minute, Fergal. When you were bringing the wheel chair down this afternoon I saw those lesions again. May I have a look?'

'What lesions?'

'Under the right humerus.'

'So where's the right humerus?' She could be irritating when she switched to nurse-speak, yet he admired it. It made her seem efficient, logical.

She put a hand under his arm and he let her raise it. 'Along here,' she explained, stroking her finger tips gently from armpit to elbow. 'Good. They're fine, completely healed. There was nothing to worry about, but they might have become a little inflamed, this weather.'

'You say something's healed before I even knew I'd got it.'

'That's how it often is, though I'd have expected you to be aware of it, in this case.'

'Aware of *what*, Mother?'

73

'That you'd rubbed against something sharp. In this area, your skin was a mass of minor abrasions and associated punctures. But very superficial. How did it happen?'

'I can't tell you how it happened when I didn't know that it had!'

'That's true. The only time I can remember seeing anything quite like it was on our honeymoon.'

'Where was it?'

He had meant: Where, on whom, had she seen this phenomenon, but she answered, 'In Suffolk. They had just reaped the corn. I was wearing sandals, and we were both in shorts. I suppose we should have kept to the lanes but naturally we didn't do that.' Her tone was wistful; she had left the kitchen and was walking through a field in Suffolk, close to her man.

A charm of finches suddenly fluttered into the garden, glided, mingled and parted, danced in airy configurations through the leaves. Fergal studied them, avoiding his mother's face. At last he said, 'So what's that got to do with minor abrasions?'

'You said? Oh, yes.' Slowly she adjusted. 'As I told you, the farmers had finished harvesting but they hadn't ploughed in the stubble. It was sharp as daggers and could penetrate like a needle, scratch quite deep. I don't know whether the straw stalks, the part they use for bedding, is any softer, but that stubble! You should have seen your father's ankles. Mine, too. Yet, like you, neither of us noticed at the time. I suppose that was understandable . . .'

But Fergal was no longer listening. A week earlier, he had fallen asleep on a bed of straw, the same that had made scratches on a girl's tanned, strong legs.

Eight

Fergal sat on his bed and gazed at the writing paper he had borrowed from his mother. Except for the address and Dear Bailey, the sheet was blank. Again he ran over an opening:

I've received your letter. I wish Striker Morrison was right but this place is dead. All the birds have flown (ha, ha.) Except there's one I keep coming across, first time was in a launderette. She was practically having a bath but she dashed off before I could take advantage. I can hear you asking, Why was she washing herself and not clothes? It was because she's sleeping out in a barn and she washed her T-shirt as well. Before you start dribbling like Groper, just get this, I haven't found her sleeping in the barn but I've got evidence to prove she does.

Another possibility was:

I haven't experimented frolicking in silage but I might try it in straw. There's a girl dosses down in a barn near here and she thought I was a chap from the Water Board. I didn't have to go in for the usual crap telling what year I'm in. She's probably a student and she's really together, she didn't turn a hair when I saw her first time in practically nothing but a bra. That was in a launderette. I'll leave that to your imagination and when you've

*finished with it if you pass it on to Groper and he goes blind it's
your responsibility not mine. She's cool enough to nick a bike,
too, after I'd cleaned it up, and go riding it round a reservoir.
(See Water Board above.)*

The girl might be afraid that he would guess it was she
who had taken the cycle, Fergal worked out, so she
couldn't admit she had seen him near the farm. That
accounted for her attempt to explain away her start of
recognition when they met in the launderette. Perhaps
she felt guilty and embarrassed. He could understand
anyone not owning up to nicking a bicycle simply in
order to ride it by the side of a reservoir.

Dear Bailey, he worked out,
*This place is weird. I'll tell you about it some other time. The
priority is the weirdest, a girl. She doesn't come from here. She
wanders around. I've met her twice and I don't know how to handle
it. That's not because I don't think I'd ever make the grade, it's
because I'm thinking she might be bonkers. Most of the time she's
laid back and she's stunning looking but she acts peculiar like
stealing rosemary from the farm garden and hoarding it in a barn and
sticking twigs of it all over the place. Mrs Helliwell, she's the woman
Mum's looking after, says rosemary means for remembrance. I can't
get my head round it, Bailey, and littering everywhere with
rosemary isn't the only crazy thing she does.*

Fergal sighed. The paper under his hand was covered in
squiggles. He could put no words on it, not before he
could write down the others: *Bailey, what you call
the incident in the river isn't history. It's like you to be*

generous but you can walk away from it, you've got nothing on your conscience. I reckon you'd be a moody sod if you were me.

Leaning against the headboard, he could feel something pressing in a back pocket. It had been there ever since it had fallen off the seat of the wheel chair. He pulled it out. The sheet of paper was thick and glossy, doubled and then pleated. Folded in this way, it reminded Fergal of a map and as he opened it, he saw that it was.

He got up, switched on the light and scrutinised it. He enjoyed maps and this one had not been published by the Ordnance Survey; it had been drawn in Indian ink, the lines fine and meticulous, the words on it written in an elegant script. Admiring the draughtsmanship, Fergal smoothed out the creases. Diagonally across them was sketched the course of a river into which ran tributary streams. Along the widest of these, Crashing Beck, was the position of houses. At the top of the map was the name: Linden, and beneath that, the signature, Matthew Bennet, M.I.C.E.

The village was small; it comprised only about three dozen houses, the church with its graveyard enclosed by a wall, and the bridge to it across Crashing Beck. Running out of the village and deeper into the valley was a lane that Fergal had walked up a few days earlier. It was marked Donkey Lane on the map and curved down to the river, over a bridge and up the opposite bank. So there was another bridge, but still covered by water.

Those who had lived in Linden were recorded; a name and a trade was written by each house. Fascinated, he read: L.P. Dingle and family, labourer; H.D. Ambler, post

79

mistress; Desmond Singleton, grocer; Walter Ibbotson and family, cabinet maker; Toby Wheatley, builder and steeple jack; Mr & Mrs Gilbert Beardsall, mechanic. Near the bridge was the house of N.S. Greaves and family, farmer. Close by was one marked Edward and Agnes Helliwell. Beside it was a miniscule anvil, the draughtsman's symbol for a forge. So Agnes Greaves Helliwell had not always lived in this farmhouse. Understandably, Fergal had not given the subject a moment's thought, but now the map told him that she had lived in two of its houses, first with her parents and later with her husband the smith. Then, as Desmond Singleton had described, everyone had been moved out and the Helliwells had come here, storing Edward's farrier tools in one of the attic rooms.

Fergal looked at Matthew Bennet's map and identified the farmhouse in which he was sitting. It was separated from Linden, the lower stretches of the becks and the river by a band of shaded blue. The high water level of the reservoir.

And below this, in a corner where the drawing ended, were a few lines of writing, but they were not in Matthew Bennet's hand. They had been done by the person who had put her initials on water-colours and Black Monday on the package containing the flute. Fergal read:

Here men come
With a map to kill loveliness,
To destroy our valley, its fields and broad trees,
To tear down our church and homes,
Setting at naught the lives of the living and the dead.

Because I fear God
I will not curse them.
But I cannot forget
Or forgive.

Fergal folded up the sheet of paper, feeling that the map was no longer a plain, scientific drawing. It had been altered by Mrs Helliwell's poem and he recalled Desmond Singleton saying: 'They shovelled us out of our homes, out of our valley, like so much horse muck,' and Gilbert Beardsall: 'We had a bellyful of that, gelignite, a time back.'

In the room below him he could hear his mother chatting as she prepared the old woman for the night. When that was finished she would call: 'There are pickles and some cold ham/beef/cheese if you'd like supper, Fergal.' Then she would sit with him while he ate and remark: 'Isn't it nice when work's over and we can relax?' But her fingers would pick at the table cloth until she could no longer hold back the confession: 'I'm not sure I've done the right thing to come to this farmhouse. Only it's not that I see much of Phil nowadays, is it? So you'd have thought it wouldn't have been any different, living here. But I miss him just the same, Fergal, I really do.'

He had never made the comment: 'You said you wanted a change,' because he realised that was not the whole reason for her taking this job. Generally he would attempt a few sympathetic noises, a meaningless encouraging remark. But not this evening. He would like a rest from his mother, just as he would like a rest from everything to do with this map. He placed it on his chest of drawers, wishing he had never found it. Then he walked down the stairs and through the kitchen. For once he'd forgo the cold ham/beef/cheese.

Outside, the walls of the stable and outhouses compressed the twilight to umber but in the open it paled, thinned by the reflection from the blonde grass and the white chips on the track. Having no goal, Fergal strolled a short distance then turned into the meadows. Behind him was the house; in front of him was the valley holding the reservoir. He sauntered across the short grass, stepped over tussocks and sudden outcrops of stone, climbed stiles or gates, hoping that soon the air and the exercise would travel up to his brain and it would give up thoughts of the map and Mrs Helliwell's poem and the girl. Why, it tapped out, keeping time with his steps, why does she dislike them so much? And why, since she does, has she left rosemary as a remembrance under the bridge?

Sheltered by a solitary ash, there was a manger round which sheep had gathered. They scattered on his approach, their hooves clipping nervously at the parched earth; one wheezed, shaking its head, like an old man gagging. Then their noise ended, sharpening the silence. Fergal leant against the manger and listened. And gradually, as if he had willed it, there came a slight susurration, a disturbance in the air like the stir of a rising breeze. He stayed his breath and stared into the sepia dusk. Again the air rustled, was shaped to a sound, fragile, then died away. He crept forward, anxious not to startle it, and found that he had reached the end of the meadow land. In the distance the trees were a dense mass, their crests black against the russet sky; at his feet was the shelf of grass and its hanging roots. He was standing where the blue shaded line had been drawn on the map.

The sound came again, clearer, was a single tremulous note. It was below him; his slanting route had brought him close to Linden and he was looking down on Crashing Beck. Not far along it, he could make out the low ruins of the church. Fergal squatted on the cracked earth, straining his ears.

The note was repeated; others were added, soft, testing, grew into phrases. There was a pause, the click of stones, a cough as a throat was cleared. Then the notes and the phrases found their place, were spun together in an unbroken thread of sound; and gradually, through the advancing darkness, a melody rose out of the ruins of Linden. It dipped and lifted, hovered and quivered, plaintive. A live thing, it spoke of abandon and solitude and its cadences were formed by tears. Until its grief was gathered into a final lamentation that gradually diminished and faded into the night.

It left an emptiness; there was nothing to take its place. The village was still, waiting for a litany, a toll of bells, while the darkness slid down the slopes then surged along the deserted street. Fergal watched; his blood thundered. The night moved, closed again as a portion detached itself, stepped laboriously through the heaped stones and stood where the darkness was thinner on the arch of the bridge. Forcing his eyes to give it shape, Fergal saw that it was a figure, one arm crooked round a slim object and the other extended, leading to a stick. After crossing the bridge, the figure walked slowly along the bank of the beck towards its head and the ruins of the mill.

For a time Fergal remained; then, his blood quieter, he rose and walked some distance along the ledge of roots before turning into the meadow grass. He could have gone in the direction the other had taken, returned to the farmhouse by Mrs Helliwell's path, but he could not risk coming upon the flute player. If he did, it would be obvious that he had heard the music and he sensed that it had not been meant for his ears.

So he forced his way through the meadows where all landmarks had vanished, covered by the night. Eventually he stumbled on to the track and as his eyes grew accustomed to its pale tape he watched it unroll ahead of him, stone by stone, to the house.

It was quiet when he entered. Both women were in their rooms and Gyp merely flicked her tail lazily; she did not yelp or move from her position outside Mrs Helliwell's door. She exerted herself no more than when others came, equally familiar. Fergal stepped over her and descended into the dairy. He had obeyed Mrs Helliwell's order, replacing the stick exactly where it had been left. Tonight it was not there. It had been collected.

Tired, he chewed through a Cornish pasty and thought: On the first night the man came, Mrs Helliwell didn't let him fetch the flute from her desk because he might have woken us as he walked up the two flights of stairs. Instead, she promised to have it delivered.

Fergal and Walter had seen to that.

Nine

The next day neither Agnes Helliwell nor Fergal referred directly to the flute player. All she said was: 'You were out roaming,' and he merely nodded.

Once he might have challenged: Why that music? What did it mean? But that day he thought: I'm not sure I want to know.

She sensed this, telling him, 'There are things have to be done and you're a brave young chap strolling round here in the dark, town bred.'

Provoked, he answered, 'I'd have thought there were more dangers in the town though there are lights.'

'You know I wasn't meaning dangers as such.'

'Yes . . . I've had a look in the dairy. The stick's gone.'

'It was needed.'

Madge had said to him: That afternoon in the sun has worked wonders. Agnes seems much more relaxed. Will you ask her if she'd like to go out again?

As before, he had doubted his mother's diagnosis and had told her silently: Mrs Helliwell's been cured by that music. Then he had wondered at the idea of 'cured'. Cured of what?

However, he asked, 'Would you like to sit in the garden again?'

Her answer was what he had predicted: 'Your mother mustn't trouble. It's not necessary now. It's given me a nice boost.'

He thought: For how long? Because, as she spoke, a nerve had flashed up her neck.

'I'm going to Niddford with the washing again,' he told her. 'Tomorrow. Mr Beardsall's going to fetch me.'

'Gilbert's not a bad fellow. I've known him since he was in short breeches.' He felt like saying: Surprise, surprise. 'Your mother's more faddy than Sonia. She lets the clothes pile up before she takes out the truck.'

'Even if I had a bike I couldn't manage the cases.'

'Ah, that bicycle. Now that *is* a mystery.' She spoke as if there were no others.

Impulsively, he began: 'I've seen . . .' then abruptly stopped. He realised that he was protecting someone but he did not know whether it was Mrs Helliwell or the girl.

'You've seen the tracks?' the old woman interpreted. 'It's a clever one, doing it without being caught.' By caught, she meant: seen. 'The rest's folly. Taking that thing so close!'

'Why?'

'Doubtless it looks bland enough, but if that bike got out of hand, things could turn nasty, especially where the river goes in. It's low, there's no escaping that, but the banks shelve sudden and the currents haven't changed. They've proved what they can do.'

That was one reason he sought the girl; he wanted to

warn her, he wanted to say: You may have a poor opinion about people living here, but it's worth taking their advice, then reporting Mrs Helliwell's comments.

Also, the irises of her eyes were freckled with gold.

So he walked up to the barn that morning but neither the girl nor the cycle was there. Bitterly he thought: She wouldn't get around as she does if she hadn't snatched it, leaving me to tramp. How does she manage to do it? How can she be so elusive? The tracks by the side of the reservoir have been seen, but not her making them. When people spend their days scanning the countryside for signs of activity! Then slamming the information straight on to the Internet. Or more likely sending up smoke signals. And what about semaphore? Morse? Sheep dogs with notes pinned to their scruffs? Pigeons? Within minutes of her being sighted careering along by the water, the whole community would have heard of it.

Had she made those inexplicable, senseless tracks – yet keeping such a precise margin from the edge – at night time? With no lamp on the cycle. He tried to remember when there had been moonlight and he could not imagine anything more desolate than the water lying stagnant below the bare slopes, their narrow ridges curving like ribs, and then the ruins of Linden, its fragments scattered pallid and lifeless under the moon.

And last night, had the grieving flute music reached her as she lay alone on this straw?

It was pricking into his denim trousers. A blanket would prevent scratches. But that evening, when he smuggled one out of the farm, the girl was not there to receive it. He laid it over the straw, placing on it a pillow he had brought from his bed.

He had decided to continue the search early the next day but he overslept and had only just finished breakfast when Gilbert Beardsall arrived. So when the man asked, 'Have you any jobs to do besides attending to the laundry?' he answered, 'Yes.' Looking for a girl.

Therefore, as soon as the clothes were swishing round in their machines, Fergal strode to the back of the launderette and knocked on the store closet door. Tracie opened it, revealing a deck chair which straddled the buckets and mops. She offered him a chocolate biscuit after he had got through his question.

'I know who you're talking about. I mean, I don't as a rule have folks asking to wash theirselves at the sink. Have you got a message you want getting to her or something?'

'I was wondering whether you knew when she'd be in here again.'

'Were you, now?' Tracie gave her version of a knowing look. 'Well, she's a nice young woman; she can't help talking posh; there's no side on her.'

'Do you know if she's coming in today?'

'She never does twice in one day.'

'So she's been here already?'

'That's what I'm saying. She was standing out there on the pavement when I opened. I said to her, You're early and she said back, I had a very comfortable night.'

He was glad he had taken the blanket, but if he hadn't, would she have arrived in Niddford later? She had entered this launderette this morning, had washed in that sink, and he had missed her. Fergal cursed silently.

'I can't say the next time she'll be here,' Tracie told him, 'but I'll tell her you were asking after her.'

Declining the offer of a consolatory mug of tea, Fergal left the launderette and searched through the town. Not until he thought he was attracting attention by dashing into shops, looking round and making no purchase, did he return and, having put the washed clothes through the drier, he carried them to the car.

'Have you finished, then?' Gilbert Beardsall asked. 'No more business outstanding? Neither have I. What a day this is, not a hint of a wind and you could fry an egg on the pavement. You'll be as glad as I am to get home.'

'Yes, but I was wondering whether you could drop me off before then.' After the failed morning he was restless; he had to keep looking. Surely the more hours he spent, the probability was that he would succeed. 'You'll be taking the car right to the farm anyway, and Mother will help with the cases.'

'No need for that. If you want dropping sooner, all you have to do is say where.'

'I'd like to walk back to the farm along the path from Crashing Beck. There's a lane to the beck, isn't there?' The one Martin Helliwell had indicated.

'There is. I'll put you down where it comes into the road. It'll bring you top side of the reservoir.' The man avoided the name, Linden.

They did not talk again until Fergal exclaimed, pointing, 'This morning I didn't see that.'

'We've come a different way.'

'Is it a piece of farm machinery? From this angle, it looks like a cross.'

'That's right.'

The width of a field and two walls separated it from the road and huge, made of wood, it stood alone without company of chapel or church.

'Who put it there?'

'Those that were left. Still above ground. It's where they brought the relics from the other graveyard.'

Wincing, Fergal asked, 'You mean they dug up the graves?'

'Well, you don't suppose what was in them could be left under water, do you? Not hygienic,' Gilbert answered, testy.

They crossed the bridge over the river and came to the end of Crashing Beck Lane. Mr Beardsall drew the car onto the grass verge. 'Don't you mind me,' he said in apology. 'It's no more easy thinking on today than it was twenty year since. Look, if you want, you can read about it, it's no state secret.' He reached to the back seat for his jacket, shook out a wallet and searched through. Eventually he found several small squares of folded newspaper and, selecting one, he handed it to Fergal. Yellowed, worn at the edges, it scattered a few whiskery flakes. 'You'll not want to read it this minute,' he instructed.

'When shall I give it back?'

'You keep it. I don't know why I haven't thrown this lot away before now. They're no use.'

Fergal slipped the billet into the pocket of his shirt and started down the lane. According to a direction carved on a stone in a wall, the distance to Linden was a mile but a fortnight here had taught him to suspect such measurements. He decided that they were less concerned with accuracy than to encourage the weary walker. He opened more buttons on his shirt and flapped it against his chest to produce a temporary breeze, but by now he hardly noticed the heat. It had persisted so long that it had become a constant phenomenon, as inevitable as day and night. He was more aware of hunger and told himself: You're not fifteen minutes away from food! Why didn't you stop for dinner before beginning another futile hunt? You won't find her near Crashing Beck. She doesn't go to the reservoir during the day.

This argument was to insure against disappointment, or to coax fate to prove it was wrong. After all, there was a chance.

The lane took him to the beck. It was shallower now and, reaching the sluices, it sieved effortfully through the cracks. Climbing down, Fergal saw that the course of water was merely a thin filament over its stones, waiting to evaporate into the air. Then for the first time he became aware that the valley was not silent and he looked towards Linden.

People were walking among its ruins, examining hearths, gazing up chimneys. Some stood on the bridge and posed for photographs; others climbed up the slopes and looked through binoculars; older sightseers rested on the stumps of orchard trees; a few picked their way through the piled stones of the church.

Fergal would have gone no further but he had come

with a purpose, so he walked into the village and, going from group to group, looked at every face. It was a fruitless search.

Stupid! he sneered at himself; it's obvious she wouldn't be here when this lot's crawling all over it. If I'd known Linden had got to be a tourist attraction and there'd be coach parties dumped every minute I wouldn't have come.

He decided to climb directly up the bank of the reservoir and cut through the woods at a point where, confident of orientation, he knew he would come to Mrs Helliwell's path. But he did not reach it. As he stepped over the lip of grass roots that had formerly fringed the reservoir's water, he found her; at last.

Ten

The girl was crouched against the bole of a fallen pine, her arms crossed over her knees. Although she must have seen him approaching, she had chosen not to flee away. Fergal sat down beside her and murmured a greeting.

Hers was: 'Thanks for the blanket; and the pillow.'

'How do you know it was me who left them?'

She smiled. 'Who else?'

What he had really meant was: Did you see me?

'They made sleeping more comfortable.'

'Tracie mentioned that.'

Her eyebrows questioned.

'When I saw her this morning. I had to go to the launderette.'

She did not ask: How did I come up in the conversation? merely, 'So you were saddled with laundry duty again?'

'I'll say; and it doesn't come in my favourite top ten of jobs.'

'You seem to be given plenty.'

She was as informed as everyone else. Fergal thought: Why don't I catch sight of these people catching sight of me? 'That's why I came here, to help Mother look after

Mrs Helliwell. At least, that was one reason.' He wanted to say: Look, I haven't spent days trying to track you down in order to discuss household chores.

The girl was thinking, crinkling her eyelids. 'So at the farm where you are it's a Mrs Helliwell?'

'Yes. Why?'

'I've heard of her, that's all,' she answered slowly. Then she nodded down to Linden. 'Just look at them.'

Fergal said, 'Where have they all come from? For a start there was nobody, well, almost nobody.' He looked at her profile but her expression did not change. 'Then suddenly there are dozens.'

'They're probably on their way to the Dales Show.'

'Could be.' Mr Singleton had mentioned it. 'I suppose they're bound to be interested.'

Not moving her eyes from the scene below them, the girl hissed, 'Ghouls.'

'You could say that.'

Yet the visitors did not deserve this description. They were a little uneasy. As they strolled among the rectangles of low walls they appeared subdued. They did not hail each other or call to children and when a dog barked suddenly it was ordered to be quiet. Chastened, it sniffed in a dispirited fashion along the bank of the beck and towards the bridge.

'I was expecting that would happen,' the girl told him, interpreting his glance. 'So I've fetched it back.' She gestured behind her and he saw the wreath of rosemary, its ribbon uncrushed and clean.

'Gyp didn't touch it.'

'I know, and I was glad you left it alone.'

'What should I do with it?'

'Stick it back in the garden, perhaps?' she teased. 'All the same, you could have interfered.'

'I didn't want to.'

'You must have thought the person who put it there was bonkers.'

'I don't know — different anyway,' he suggested tactfully.

He was thinking: She doesn't ask for a summary of my life to date, all the usual stuff, the teams I'm in, and wanting a list of previous girls. (Ha! ha!) It's as if we've already got through all that.

This ease was not only in their conversation. The girl had laid out clothes to dry and, turning them over, said, 'Would you, please?' She indicated a bra and pants out of her reach. As Fergal rearranged them on the grass, she said, 'Thanks, Fergal. I can see they aren't cooked yet. I like things well grilled, not medium rare.'

'How do you know my name's Fergal?'

'There's a letter for you in the tin at the gate.'

'I would've looked, only Mr Beardsall dropped me off earlier. What's yours?'

'My name? Alex.'

She pulled the rosemary onto her lap, bringing its fragrance. 'It's beginning to look as if it'll be past its sell-by date soon. In any case, I shouldn't have put it there. But I hadn't the patience. I just bunged it under the only bridge there was.'

He wanted to ask: Do you bung rosemary

under bridges for kicks or something?

She added, 'I was sorry, though, that it was the wrong one.' Her tone was as matter of fact as if she had said: I caught the wrong bus.

So he heard himself explaining: 'The other bridge must be way under the reservoir.' He visualised the drawing he had found. 'See those two lines of stones running out of the village? They must have been walls along Donkey Lane. If you look opposite in a diagonal across the reservoir you can see it continues up the hill-side.' The stripe of earth was smooth and packed hard. Fawn against the grey coloured slope, it was still visible after years under water. 'If you imagine a line between the two stretches of the lane and bring another down from those little waterfalls on the river up there, where they intersect will be the bridge.'

Alex nodded, smiling at his meticulous description. 'Yes, I know. But it's not on the maps.' Her statement asked him where he had found his information.

'I've seen an old drawing.'

'So have I.' Her expression turned sombre. Then she grumbled, 'By now you'd expect that bridge to be showing.'

'There might be something. I think I can make out a break in the reflection coming off the water, but it's a long way out. I couldn't swear to it, not without binoculars.' His father had not sent them; he must give him a ring.

'I wonder how much longer it's going to take.'

'To do what?'

'To go down enough for the bridge to show.'

'Let's hope the drought lets up before then.'

'No! Not yet! Not now it has begun. I have to see that bridge. Close. Stand on it. I've waited.' She spoke with a passion that reminded him of her words: I wouldn't live anywhere near this lot.

He began to warn, 'You have to be careful. There's still a lot of water there and it's not only the depth you have to consider, it's –' but he was interrupted.

There was a shriek below them. It was followed by shouts and the piercing repetitions of a name. The sightseers halted, their heads swinging round as a woman pushed through them, screeching, pointing, hampered by a buggy from whose handle bobbed a large silver balloon. This picture was still in frame when another overlaid it and Fergal and Alex had leaped over the sill of roots, had landed on the baked slope and were racing down to the reservoir where a small child stood half immersed, the water circling his waist.

Although the ground appeared to be concrete hard, it was difficult to run fast. The bank was uneven, broken by clefts of vanished rills, and the thick dust refused to be gripped by their trainers. They skidded, scoring out furrows, harassed by the sound of the child's frenzied wails. Seeing them, he lifted up his arms, tottered, then recovered.

'Don't move. Stay where you are,' Alex shouted.

Then a man who had been sprinting by the side of the reservoir reached him first, hoisted the child onto his chest and waded back. 'He's had a bad scare,' he panted.

97

'Nothing a dry pair of trousers won't put right. Blimey! Puffs you, doesn't it, a good gallop?'

Fergal nodded. But it wasn't the running that had caused him to lose breath. It was the sight of the child locked in the water, turning his face to him, frightened, then the terror of them both when he almost fell.

As he and Alex climbed up the slope, he said, 'I'm glad he didn't go under.'

'Yeh. I bet the water's perishing.'

'I could've coped with that.'

'So?'

'I just wouldn't have liked thrashing about trying to get hold of him.'

'No more would I. Can't you swim?'

'Of course I can swim.'

'You look as if you'd be good at it.'

'I'm not bad.' He wasn't going to mention the certificates his mother treasured. 'I just wouldn't have liked trying to get hold of him, that's all,' he repeated. He was dangerously close to telling her about the 'incident in the river.'

'But you would have.'

'I suppose so.'

She was looking at him, puzzled. 'There's no suppose about it. You belted down there faster than me. You wouldn't have hesitated a single second if he'd dropped in, been swept away – though the surface is so still, that's hard to imagine. But say he had, you'd have jumped in and swum out, same as me.'

'Yes.' He could not admit: I can't guarantee it.

Two months ago, yes, but not now.

In answer to the child's howling, his thoughts had screamed; Don't go under. For my sake, please don't go under and drift away.

They had reached the grass and the neat line of her clothes. She gathered them up, laid them in her rucksack, then the bunch of rosemary. 'I'm going now,' she told him. 'The A level results are out tomorrow and there'll be stuff to see to. It'll be Sunday at the earliest before I can get back. Let's hope the other bridge will be out of the water by then.'

Delighted that she was not about to disappear for ever, he offered, 'I'll look out for it. Though that won't make any difference,' and they laughed.

'How's it got to that time?' she said, looking at her watch. 'I have to be on the Niddford road in forty minutes.'

'No hassle. You'll easily manage. Are you catching a bus?'

'A friend's picking me up. Her family are on their way home from holiday.'

Swinging her rucksack on to his shoulder, he let her look for another minute at the unrippling water, searching, before he said, 'Hey!' and preceded her through the trees.

'Liz said they could meet me earlier but I wanted to make sure that the reservoir hadn't stopped shrinking.'

'It can't do anything else till there's rain.'

'I know, but I have to keep checking. That's why I had to borrow the bike again; I was using it to prove the water was still going down.' Referring to the bicycle she showed no embarrassment; it seemed that 'borrowing' it was excused by her need. 'That was stupid, I admit, you can see the level's dropping without making a record with lines of tyre marks to compare.'

'I saw them. And they haven't gone.' The tracks had been under his feet as he watched the man rescue the child. 'There's been nothing to wash them away.'

'And won't be yet, I hope. But can you imagine where I got the idea from, for making the marks? From my mother. I used to adore coke years ago and Mum would draw a line round the bottle to see how much of it I'd drunk. It never occurred to her that I could rub her mark out and put another at the new level. I thought it was marvellous, her not suspecting, till I started to feel rotten about it.'

So she went on and Fergal was reminded of a neighbour who would corner him for hours, urgent to talk to a living face rather than to the deaf photographs in her silent rooms. And it struck him that Alex was lonely, like Mrs Simon. As he had been. Perhaps that was why she had been watching him, observing what he did. Just as he had searched for her, thinking about her for days.

But when they reached Mrs Helliwell's path she told him, 'I'll take the pack now. You don't have to come any further. Please, I would rather you didn't. It's not far to the road.'

'Best of luck with the results, then.'

He watched until the shadows of the trees closed round her. *She may be out of her head, Bailey,* he added a postscript to the letter he had thought out. *She's got a fixation about bridges and decorating them with herbs but I can take that on board. Because as well as being a cracker, she's got guts; she wouldn't be stopped if she'd made up her mind to do something.*

The idea excited him. She's a bit like you are, he told Bailey: reckless. I'll have to make sure she doesn't come to any harm. Which means I'll have to manage better than I did with you.

Immediately he entered the farm house, Mrs Helliwell's bell fetched him to her room.

'I never knew it could take such a time from Crashing Beck Lane,' she told him.

Irritated, he answered, 'Depends how fast you walk.'

'Now then, don't take on. It's only natural Gilbert Beardsall should mention where he dropped you off.'

Silently Fergal corrected: Not mention – report back.

'Your dinner's being kept warm in the oven. Madge has gone down the track for the post.'

'Good. There's a letter for me.' He paused, enjoying her confusion and the unspoken question: How do you know? 'According to my informant.'

'Your . . .' Her cheeks twitched, under the sheet a foot pounded and the laughter surged. 'That takes some beating,' she croaked.

He grinned. 'Watch this space.'

'It's not often anyone gives me a laugh. It's better than the pills, hearing a young fellow joking.'

'I wasn't joking.'

'Is that so? As a rule we don't have anyone interfering

with that post tin but it could tempt peepers. Still, that's no cause to put a lock on it.'

'What would be the use? You'd leave it open, wouldn't you? For those without a key.'

'I'm not certain that tin comes into the same category as the back door, but I'll think on. You're droll today, Fergal. I'm beginning to wonder what went on at Niddford.'

'Not a lot.'

'I doubt that. Now you'll spare me another word? You've been walking and there's things you can't miss. I'm told there's cars parked past the lane end.'

'Yes. There were people, looking.'

'They're after sensation; that's what they want. Heathens!' Then she muttered, 'Hoping to see Donkey Lane bridge.'

'I'd be glad if you'd do something for me,' she addressed Fergal. 'No, not now, nor yet tomorrow. Sunday would be a proper time.'

Alex had said she might return on Sunday. 'Would it take long?' The question sounded discourteous and he blushed.

'So there *were* more attractions in Niddford than a laundry! What I have in mind won't put stop to a lady friend.'

'I didn't say I wouldn't do it.'

'No, and I'll see you're not put out. It's time you had that dinner. If it weren't for all that muscle you'll look wizened. We'll deal with the other job when we come to it.'

Fergal took a dish of lasagne out of the oven and for seven minutes gave it his full attention. After that he could tackle a treacle sponge less urgently and reflect on the day. He played back his meeting with Alex, ran it through several times, found no private embarrassments, and pronounced it a success.

Moving to less personal details, he was led back to Mrs Helliwell. Both she and Alex expressed similar disgust at the sightseers and they shared an obsession with the retreating water. However, the old woman feared what it was revealing whereas Alex desired it. She had insisted: 'I have to see that bridge. Close. Stand on it. I've waited.' Over Donkey Lane bridge, she and Mrs Helliwell were completely opposed.

'Well, Watson, what do you make of it?' he asked Gyp.

She had come into the kitchen and Fergal realised that some time earlier he had seen her dash out, her feathery tail waving excitedly. He had assumed his mother was approaching and now leaving the table, he walked into the yard.

There was no sign of his mother; it was not she that Gyp had welcomed. Placed to lean against the stable door, its chrome sparkling in the sun, was the bicycle.

Eleven

The first thing Fergal did was look at his watch. In five minutes Alex should be at the meeting place with Liz, yet she had spent precious time bringing the cycle to the farm. He pushed it out of the yard and went straight up through the plantation, lugging it round fallen trees, riding it when he could. At the stile with the flag steps, he carried the bike over his head, then shoved it laboriously through the meadow grass. Reaching the gate, he wheeled it through and on to the lane. It was empty.

Relieved that Alex had not missed her lift but disappointed, he stood for a moment wondering why he had come. Liz would have waited if Alex were late but had there been a hitch in the arrangements, he could hardly have taken her to a train. He imagined her sitting on the handle bars while he pushed at the pedals. It was years since he and Bailey had done that. And never on a cycle as antiquated as this.

But it worked, and she had given it back, or lent it, no matter which, and gripping the handle bars he cantered as if he were starting a motor bike, threw a leg over, bounced onto the saddle and pedalled like a maniac down the lane. He didn't care where he went; it was enough to be moving fast. Or, rather: faster than he could run. Trees and gates didn't exactly flash by, but it didn't take so long to pass them and though the tarmac could have been smoother, it was not scattered with pine cones or fallen branches or knobbed with bits of rock. Exhilarated, shouting, 'Watch out Formula One, here I come,' he skidded round a bend, careered along the road to the dam, tacked across it without as much as a glance at the water, and puffed up the hill so that just for the hell of it he could free-wheel down. Then once more on level ground, he went through a number of the old routines that had once been obligatory: he left the pedals dangling while he squatted on the saddle, trainers hooked over the crossbar; he drew his feet back, squeezed them under his buttocks and took the bike in tight circles; he swung himself round and steered facing the back wheel.

By the time he made his way home – a wave to Desmond Singleton's Village Store and Post Office; much swearing at the loose chips on the track – he was ready to take anything on. Riding, he created a breeze that cooled his skin; his muscles tingled, and he put aside the mysteries of Linden, the insidious threat of Donkey Lane bridge and Alex's interest in it. When Madge handed him the letter, his disappointment that it was not Bailey's handwriting on the envelope soon passed. He winked and tapped his nose at her question: Where did you find the bicycle? Deciding to take a bath, he did not fret at the labour but simply replenished the boiler, waited for the water to heat and ferried it in buckets to the bathroom. He was thinking of Alex's smile, her laughter and the burnishing sun in her hair.

Lying in foam produced from one of his mother's bottles, he opened the letter. Madge had said, 'I can see this is from Phil. I hope he's got the one I gave you to post.'

'That was last night, Mother! He hasn't got a crystal ball. I posted it at the office in Niddford this morning.'

'Did you? Was that only today?' Miserable, she added, 'Writing it must have taken longer than I thought.'

It seemed that neither of his parents shared Bailey's commitment to brevity. His father's letter ran to two pages. He reported:

'I rang that sister of yours on Sunday. She's enjoying the work experience but she's pretty exhausted. When I suggested mildly that she should take a holiday, she nearly blew up. That, she told me, was all she needed! Sounded like a contradiction to me but I didn't press the point.'

There was a paragraph about making a meal:

'I was in early yesterday and decided to tackle a "simple snack", the recipe book's description. Cooking and preparation time was supposed to take twenty minutes. It was lucky I didn't try anything from the Advanced Gourmet section. The "snack" and I didn't come together over a can of lager until nearly midnight.'

He described an evening he had spent with a friend, asked questions about the farm, Mrs Helliwell, and hoped that Madge had not taken on too much.

'She can go beyond her strength just as Lorna does, but I don't need to remind you of that. I'm sure you'll be helping her with the heavy work.

'And how are you occupying yourself? I'm amazed that you've suddenly taken up bird watching. Or am I wrong? I refer to your request for your grandfather Collins's binoculars. Thanks for the card. I haven't forgotten, and I've thought that, instead of sending them, I could drive up. I'm not inviting myself to the farm. That may not be convenient, I'm sure Madge will be busy, but I could take you out to lunch. This may sound an elaborate arrangement just to hand over a pair of binoculars but I'd be pleased to see something of that part of the world and it would be a chance for you to pass on your news. I've nothing on either Saturday or Sunday. Give me a ring to let me know how you feel, and remember me to your mother. All the best, Dad.'

Fergal folded up the damp sheets and dropped them beside the bucket. 'You're right, Dad,' he told him. 'A four-hour drive to bring a pair of binoculars is definitely elaborate, especially when you seem to think it's necessary to keep out of Mother's way. Is it? I don't know about that, but I do know your arrangement is as complicated as any Bailey would dream up for an excuse to run into a girl. I think that's what you're after. You're trying to manoeuvre seeing Mother.'

His guess was confirmed at the end of his telephone call to Philip. They had agreed to meet on Saturday and had decided that Philip should pick up Fergal at the gate to the farm track. 'Don't worry, I'll find it,' Philip had assured him.

Then he said, 'I don't think I should drop you off later than six in view of my having the journey home.'

'Right.'

'So I'll leave you at the gate at six,' his father repeated and added with ponderous emphasis, 'No doubt Madge will want to know what time to expect you back.'

I was right, Fergal congratulated himself, grinning into the mouthpiece. And now he's asking me to make a date for him.

'Did you hear that, Mother?' he called loudly although she was only five paces away. 'Dad says to tell you I'll be back at the gate at six o'clock.'

Simultaneously down the line and across the kitchen they answered, 'Fergal, that's enough.'

'Sorry,' he told them both. 'Just testing,' and he put down the handset, wondering how two grown adults could be so ridiculous.

'Really!' Madge exclaimed, cross, then: 'Gyp's asking for a walk.'

She nodded towards the dog who stood at the door, all begging eyes and thrashing tail.

'If you want to get rid of me, why don't you say so, Mother? We'll be in the meadows at the front, so all you have to do is give a shout if you want anything done.'

He enjoyed her answering glare.

It had been a good day, Fergal decided as he walked through the meadows; at least, since he had found Alex. He had almost forgotten about the hunt in Niddford, the return journey with Mr Beardsall and that huge cross in a field. Looking over graves where they had interred mouldering bodies and bundles of bones.

He felt in his shirt pocket, took out the threadbare newspaper cutting and gently unfolded it. From Mr Beardsall's saying 'You can read about it, it's no state secret,' he had expected an account of the transfer of graves from Linden church yard, but the man had made a mistake and given him a different report. What Fergal read was:

STEEPLEJACK TOBY'S LAST TUNE

Another dramatic episode in the Linden Valley reservoir construction saga has occurred only hours after divers had brought up a body. Bystanders stood amazed at the sight of a man swimming across the reservoir which filled steadily after the official Grand Closing of the dam.

Mr Needham, garage owner, who had made a fifty-mile journey specially to gaze upon this incredible feat of civil engineering, told our reporter: 'I had brought my family and several friends in a mini bus, we were making a day of it, and the first thing to catch our eyes was this person in the water.' Mr Needham's immediate thought was the individual had fallen in and he offered to telephone the fire brigade, but an onlooker assured him, 'Toby Wheatley knows what he's about.'

Mr Needham considered that it was a really peculiar thing, the area was crowded, people had come miles but, he pointed out eloquently, 'You could hear a pin drop.' He thought it was a dare and the swimmer intended to swim right across but he was aiming for the church steeple. For readers not acquainted with the latest news, the steeple projects several feet out of the water due to an error in calculation.

110

There was speculation among the watchers regarding the pack fastened to the intrepid swimmer's shoulders. On enquiry among the locals identified at the back of the crowds, it transpired that Mr Wheatley was a steeplejack. One person claimed, 'He knows that steeple better than his own face.' Mr Wheatley was then seen to remove belts and straps from his pack and secure himself to the steeple which is a prominent landmark in the reservoir. When asked if he could explain this extraordinary behaviour, the speaker replied to your reporter, 'Wait on.'

No individual, not even Old Moore in his almanack could have predicted what followed next. After he was attached to the steeple, Mr Wheatley took some tubes out of his pack. After fitting them together he began to play them. According to a visitor on the spot, the instrument Steeplejack Wheatley was playing was a flute. Your reporter questioned one of the local bystanders regarding this peculiar incident but he declined to comment. One of the members of Mr Needham's party said it reminded her of a hymn but she thought that there were bits of the tune added on. It could be said that it put a damper on the proceedings which were not improved when it was noted that the locals had taken off their hats. Most of the spectators followed suit and returned to their cars.

Your reporter waited until Steeplejack Wheatley swam back but when asked if he played the flute regularly he only answered 'Not any more.' That was all that could be elicited as friends took over to dry his dripping frame and give him warm soup from a thermos. We trust that he will soon recover from his ordeal.

The inquest on the drowned man whose name is not available until his widow can be contacted will take place *tomorrow. He is believed to have met his death only hours before the reservoir began to fill.*

Fergal read the report a second time before folding up the paper. Then he called Gyp and returned to the house thinking: They all knew what was going on, the people the journalist referred to as 'locals', but they wouldn't explain. Then they doffed their hats. Could Toby Wheatley's playing have been connected with the drowned man?

They were guarding some knowledge and Mrs Helliwell seemed to be at the centre of it because the flute had been in her charge. And Toby Wheatley had broken his resolution not to play it again. Fergal had heard him two nights before. He wished that he could ask Mrs Helliwell to explain the reason; but that was impossible.

It was just as impossible for him to tell her who had been using the bike. When he went to her later that evening and she said, 'I hear you've got the bicycle,' all he answered was: 'Yes. It's come back.' It's none of her business to learn who had taken it, he decided; and I'm not letting myself be persuaded to tell her anything that might compromise Alex.

He repeated, 'Yes, it's come back. It was left in the yard,' and he stared at her, telling her that he, too, had subjects he would not discuss.

She nodded, understanding. Her only comment was, 'I didn't doubt it would be returned after the need had passed. Now you'll be able to get a way further. I wouldn't mind being on the crossbar when you go down these hills.'

'I have to get up them first,' he answered and they both laughed.

As he replenished the water in her carafe, he told her, 'Mum says don't drink this for a few minutes; it's not absolutely cold. She's boiled it. The pump's bringing up dirt and stuff and she's worried about infections.'

For a moment Mrs Helliwell was cackling, her thin body pulsing. She gasped, 'And we've been drinking it years. What stuff?'

'Worms mainly. And there's things like centipedes and kinds of beetles.'

'Then the spring's finishing,' she told him. The laughter had ended. 'How often do you pump up?'

'Twice usually, but I've done it three times today.'

'I've never known it go dry.'

'What'll happen if it does?'

'I'd have to speak to Gilbert Beardsall, see if he could cart some drums over. We'd manage. But since this spring's going, others will be going, too. So we can stop hoping.' She paused then asked abruptly. 'Do you believe God punishes, Fergal?'

Taken aback, he stuttered. 'I don't know.'

'Well, I do, and I think that is justice. The only quarrel I have with it is: I wish He'd decide and have done with it, not keep you bobbing like a yo-yo, up and down on a piece of string.'

Twelve

Impatient to see Alex, Fergal was glad of the arrangement
with his father. It would fill up a day of time that was
empty until she returned. Make that Sunday, he pleaded
to the cobalt sky and the scorched brittle grass; don't let
her be away any longer.

'You've completely exhausted that dog,' Madge
rebuked him. 'Look at her. Why in heaven's name have
you spent so many hours cycling in this heat?'

'She easily keeps up. I can't go very fast.'

'There's a real danger of sun stroke.'

'Not with all that hair on her. It's inches thick.'

'Don't prevaricate.' That was her favourite word when
she suspected she was losing an argument.

He answered, 'Oh, you've switched to me, have you?
I thought you were bothered about Gyp.'

'You should wear a hat.'

'I haven't brought one.'

'We can improvise.'

'If you mean tying knots in the corners of a hanky for
me to stick on my head, don't even begin to think about
it, Mum.'

'Perhaps Agnes could lend you something.'

'The same goes for a straw hat with silk flowers on it.'

'Not if it were left to me.' Madge sighed extravagantly.

'I wish you'd concentrate on something a bit more important. Like water. This morning I could feel there was less coming up when I pumped. I don't know whether there'll be enough till Mr Beardsall comes.'

'That's this afternoon, he expects. I'll be careful. That reminds me. Yesterday Agnes was telling me about the time they flooded the valley. Do you know anything about it?'

'A bit.'

'I see. You two do seem to get on.' Her answer held a hint of jealousy.

'Mrs Helliwell hasn't told me. Mr Singleton at the shop and Mr Beardsall have mentioned it.'

'Well, there was an outcry when it was decided to build the reservoir and it would cover the village. There were formal petitions and discussions in the papers and so forth, but it didn't stop there. The people living in the village and everybody from round about tried to prevent the contractors coming in; they blocked the roads, and the farmers wouldn't let them on the land, and they herded hundreds of cows and sheep into the valley – I forget why. Anyway, everyone was terribly worked up, emotional, and I suspect there was a lot of bad blood towards the contractors, though Agnes didn't directly say. But she did tell me that shopkeepers in Niddford refused to serve the workmen. The people here couldn't win, of course, and eventually the building started. Everyone had to move out and Agnes and Edward – he died some years ago – came here.

'But what she told me that I really can't get out of my mind is about something that happened after the dam had been closed.'

Fergal wondered whether his mother was about to describe Toby Wheatley's swim, but she did not refer to it. Presumably Mrs Helliwell had censored the episode. Madge told him, 'They had to let the water out again to demolish the church. Have you heard they had another service in it before that was done?'

'No.'

'Everybody who had lived in the village and from all the farms round turned up. It was because somebody had drowned just before the reservoir began to fill – the first time, I mean. Agnes didn't go into details, but they weren't able to bury the body in the old graveyard. It had to be taken to the one where the other graves had been moved to.'

'That's in a field on the other side of the reservoir.'

'I thought you might have come across it. But isn't it weird, Fergal, having a memorial service in the church when it'd been under water? The pews and all the movable things had been removed but the building had been submerged and the walls were dripping.'

He didn't wish to hear. 'Why did she tell you?'

'Why shouldn't she? I get the impression that Agnes is quite upset at the reservoir's emptying. I really must make time to have a look. It's bringing back memories for her. And I'm not surprised. Imagine being at a service in a church that's been under water and you're standing where there have been gallons right up to the roof. Just

117

thinking about it is enough to make me feel suffocated.'

'So don't.'

'It isn't so simple, controlling your imagination.' Flinching, he thought: She's telling *me*! 'But here we are talking and you have to be down by the gate at one o'clock.'

'There's plenty of time.'

'Please don't leave it to the last moment. It wouldn't be nice if Philip had to wait.' She stared out of the window as if, despite the distance and the track's undulations, she might catch sight of the car. 'Have you got everything?'

He looked down at himself: trainers, denims and T-shirt. 'I can't see anything's missing.'

'Your tartan shirt might have been better.'

'Better for what? Look, Mother, all I'm doing is going out for lunch with Dad. It isn't a date.' Hearing his last words, he thought: That's how she sees it; I'm her substitute. She'd like to be the one smartening up to meet Dad.

'Well, give him my . . . Say I hope he's . . . managing.'

Philip was already in the lane, sitting by the car, when Fergal came off the track. 'No, you aren't late,' he said as Fergal looked at his watch. 'The journey took less time than I calculated. Everything in hand?' He thumbed in the direction of the farmhouse.

'More or less.'

'Like that, is it? Before we go on, let's decide about lunch. I've been told where there's a nice pub. Is that all right?'

'Yes. Who told?'

'The owner of an antique shop in Niddford. Have you noticed it when you've been in the town?'

'Yes.'

'It's full of the sort of stuff your grandmother would have called plain second-hand or junk, but there was a very pretty little picture in water-colour done by a local artist. I did wonder whether Madge might like it as a sort of memento of this month. The chap kept reducing the price as if he was trying to get rid of hot goods. Odd, considering what it was.'

Even Crispin Farnley did not wish to be reminded of Linden. Fergal said, 'Mrs Helliwell painted it. There are dozens upstairs in the attic.'

So he told Philip about the village and how it had been submerged.

'Have you had a look at it?'

'Yes, and it's creepy. The stones haven't moved or anything and there are fireplaces and stumps of trees that were in gardens; you can see how some of them grew up the walls.'

'I can understand how that makes you feel. There was a house not far from where we lived when I was a kid that had been bombed during the war. Nobody had done anything about it, I don't know why, except to put locks on the gates and board up the ground floor. It was still like that years after the war had ended and naturally we kids weren't stopped by chains on gates and boards across windows and we used to have a high old time. How we didn't come to grief I shall never know. The staircase stopped in mid air and one of our games was banging on the walls to bring down more bricks. But we stopped going, not because we'd been found out and ordered to stay away. It was that one day after school we were messing about, moving some of the bricks for some reason I can't remember, in what must have been the kitchen, and underneath them we found a purse. It was made of thin leather and was damp and mouldy and closed by a verdigris clasp. One of us opened it – it was Tim Birchell – and inside was a conker. It had green mould on it, too. Tim polished it on his sleeve and it came up bright again, and he pulled the string taut; it was held in the nut with a big double knot. I can remember to this day how we all squatted round that conker looking at it and nobody speaking. Then Tim put it back in the purse and we buried it under the bricks and ran off. We never played in that house again.'

They were silent, Philip busy with parking for they had reached the public house, Fergal absorbing the story and relating it to Linden. He might have told his father something of the rest, about the flute player and the drowned man and what Alex had done, but suddenly he was not inclined to. He decided he would take a holiday from it. Sitting outside the public house shaded by sycamores and watching the flittering chaffinches, he felt lazy and at ease. In describing the wrecked house, Philip had created an understanding between them.

Therefore he did not shrug away Philip's question: 'And what about you, Fergal? I've the impression things aren't so good at the moment.'

'You could say that.'

'Anything I can do?'

'I don't think so, Dad.'

'Can you tell me one thing? Is it something at school?'

'No, it isn't.'

'Or any trouble with the police?'

'Crikey, Dad, have you gone barmy? The boys in blue take the day off when they see me coming, and it's the same with everything else. Things just switch into boring mode when I'm there. Last time Linda Metheringham went to her grandma's they had a fire in the kitchen.'

'How did that happen?'

'Linda left the chip pan on.'

Philip smiled. 'I think I'd rather be safe than singed.'

'So would I, and that's exactly what I'm saying. Do you know, when Mum's frying chips I go into our kitchen and check the pan.'

'I'd say it's not necessary for you to feel responsible.'

'I just can't help it, and I'll tell you something else. If anyone wants a mate to go to the dentist with, or an old biddy wants her shopping carried, or Brenda Scott wants to unload about her horrible mother, they choose me.'

'It sounds as if you have an eventful time.'

'I'm not exaggerating. Well, not a lot. What I'm telling you is, nobody'd choose me if he wanted to cross the Atlantic in a hot air balloon.'

'I think you'd be a decent choice. I certainly know whom I would *not* choose.'

'Who?'

'Linda Metheringham.'

Their laughter turned heads and scattered the scavenging sparrows.

They had finished their ham salads and Fergal had begun a dish of apple crumble when Philip said, 'Don't imagine you're not appreciated. I was very glad when you said you'd come here with Madge. How is she? I haven't heard.'

'She's written a letter. I posted it on Thursday, first class.'

'I didn't receive it yesterday. This morning I left before the delivery.'

'It'll be a good read when you get it, Dad. It was bulky.'

This failed to cheer him. 'It's my fault she took on that job. You know that?'

'She said she wanted a change.'

'But not why?'

'No.' He was not sure they should be talking about his mother.

'I give too much time to the firm, Fergal, that's why. Madge feels neglected.'

'She seems all right.'

Philip shook his head. 'That's why she came here, feeling like that. She's said to me several times, "You don't need me; I'm redundant," but I didn't pay it proper attention. Except once I remember saying, "Well, find something to occupy you outside the house." How hurtful can you get? That's not easy at her age.'

'You don't have to tell me about it.'

'I want to. The point I'm making is, I didn't listen.

And that isn't, or wasn't, our way of going on. Not at first. Her coming here has made me think. It's brought me up sharp.'

'She keeps saying she's missing you,' Fergal tried.

'Does she?' Philip brightened momentarily, then: 'I don't deserve that. I've let her down.'

'Dad!'

But Philip went on relentlessly as if compelled to confess. 'Yes, I mean that. Not in material things but the ones we got married for. Like sharing. Giving support. That's what she valued. We both did. That's what I mean when I say I've let her down. Makes me feel bloody.'

They were silent. Fergal wanted to tell him: I know how you feel, Dad; not in the way you're talking about but I know what it feels like to let someone down.

He had done that to Bailey. He had failed just at the moment Bailey needed his help. And now all he could say to his father was: 'I think Mother'll get over it.'

'I hope so. It's possible. She's a generous woman. Shall I tell you something, Fergal? Don't think I'm wallowing in self pity when I say it: other people might let you off the hook but it's hard learning to forgive yourself.'

'Yes,' Fergal agreed and this time he was able to say, 'I know what you mean.'

Philip looked at him and shed his own concerns. The skin under his eyes quivered and he sat absolutely still, ready to listen.

For several minutes Fergal struggled. He would have liked to confide and his father had shown him that it could be done. But sweat started at the memories and his tongue went dry.

Finally Philip said, 'Shall we go for a stroll? I need some exercise before driving back.'

The stroll was a rapid two hour march by the end of which their shirts were soaked and their skin itched under the denims.

'If Mum could see us, she'd have a fit,' Fergal remarked as they returned to the car. 'She went on at me this morning about sun stroke.'

'By the time we get back we'll have dried out.' Catching Fergal's smile, he laughed. 'That'll save any fuss. When did we say I'd drop you off?'

'Oh, come on, Dad. You know as well as I do. It's all set up. Mum'll be there.'

And she was, a tidy figure sitting in the grass by the farm gate. There were a few seconds of:

'You're looking good, Madge,'

and 'I was just taking a walk,'

and 'It doesn't get any cooler,'

and 'Where did you go for lunch?'

and 'Thanks a lot, Dad. Be seeing you,'

and the call 'Oh, Fergal! Mr Beardsall's brought water and there's something else he delivered. It's in the dairy for you to attend to.'

Then he was walking down the track thinking how they had looked at each other, tentative, uncertain. And gradually the images in his eyes trembled, rippled, became reflections in water, were transmuted to himself and Alex; and he heard his voice tell her: 'I'm glad you're back.'

Tomorrow was Sunday. Would he see her then?

As he crossed the yard and entered the farmhouse, he encouraged himself, 'She'll be back for sure; she's got that fixation about seeing Donkey Lane bridge.'

There were empty drums stacked in a corner of the kitchen; Mr Beardsall had replenished the tank. He had also delivered something for Fergal to attend to.

He opened the door of the dairy, walked down the steps and saw, placed beside a carton of rusted tools, its white spathes like velvet in the dusky light, a hoop of lilies. A wreath.

Thirteen

He was sinking into a vast waveless lake under the accusing finger of a spire. Finding the bottom, his toes combed through sand. It gushed up, made a gritty mist round his head that blindfolded his eyes, but always his ears were full of the sound of water. It fell rhythmically, phrased to the distant melody of a flute, then it dripped down stones, ran over ledges and sills, and gathered into rivulets along the wet floor. When they came to a certain spot these parted, curved round and reformed. Curious to learn what lay in the path of these streams, Fergal tried to move forward but was restrained by the swirling sand and the water which bore down upon him, bowing his shoulders, expelling the faraway music from his ears and packing them with its own insistent roar.

Before he looked at the place where the streams parted then joined, he must reach what he came for. Behind this barrier of water there were arms that thrashed, snared; while his own muscles would not flex; his lungs were bulging, bruising his ribs; his skull creaked, ready to crack.

Exhausted, he leant against a stone font. The water in it was not heavy, his cupped hand slid through it easily; it polished his fingers to silk. But it was vanishing, leaving at

127

the bottom centipedes, knots of worms. Among them a fish flapped, a wire hooked in a gill, its mouth pulsing, its eye staring up. Then a hand that was not his own stretched forward, unlatched the wire and calmed the flicking tail. Released, the fish drifted away and Fergal tried to follow but, though he ran swiftly, he covered no ground until he was in a wheelchair which took him to the place where the streams parted. They were curling round a wreath of white flowers. And in the dripping place that had been drowned and resurrected there was a low sad dirge whispering from many mouths. When that was finished the streams of water came together and carried the flowers away.

But a spray remained, green, without blossoms, and gliding through the silver striped leaves was the fish. Its eyes were lustrous and forgiving; they belonged to Bailey. Fergal would have addressed him but the streams grew deeper, their flow quickened, toppling the wheelchair. As he fought against the current, struggling for consciousness, to master the dream to end, Fergal looked down through the water and saw the tracks of a bicycle that had passed over the sand on the nave's floor.

It was early morning. The fluid that had covered his body was sweat. His mind still travelling the country of his dream, Fergal's eyes registered the stripe of sun that lay across his bed. Pushing the sheet away, he saw something move against the window. He stared, puzzled, then understood that the curtains were wrinkling in the breath of a light draught. Slowly he considered this novelty. Always the curtains had hung unstirring. Did this small breeze herald the coming of rain?

He rose and looked out, examining the sky. It had not altered, a dome of unblemished blue. Beneath it, a mist gauzed the meadows and laced through the trees.

There were no noises or smells from the kitchen. His mother had not yet got up. Because it was Sunday. Sunday! Then he was pulling on denims, trainers, selecting a clean T-shirt, while in the room under him there was a cough and the whine of a dog.

'It seems Mother's having a lie in,' he told Mrs Helliwell ten minutes later. 'I've brought you a cup of tea.'

Seeing her struggle to pull the sheet up to her throat, he recalled that he had never come to her until she was washed and dressed in day clothing. Careful to show that he was not sneaking a look, he placed the tea on the table beside the bed.

'What a nice thought, Fergal. I could do with that. The only thing is, I don't reckon I can reach it.'

They regarded each other, indecisive. At last she said, 'I suppose I've got to ask you to lift me up.'

'No hassle.' He was prompt, brisk, collecting the pillows and cushions, while he thought: Why did she have to blush?

'That's lovely,' she thanked him. 'It's not easy, shifting a dead weight.'

'Any time.' The weight had been nothing, but levering her up, holding the skinny arms, he had feared that the bird bones might snap in his grasp.

Agnes stuck the straw in her cup and sucked noisily. 'I don't think it's so much a case of Madge having a lie in as you rising early,' she commented. 'Going by the clock.'

For the first time that morning he looked at his watch. 'I had a dream, woke myself out of it.'

'It wasn't wanted?'

'I didn't like it.' Because she had allowed him to lift her, he could say, 'It was happening in the church, before the water was let out so that they could demolish it.'

'Ah. I've no doubt there's a lot have dreams of that. But it isn't for you to dream about.' Then, putting the subject from her, she added, almost mischievous, 'You've got other things. Isn't it today you're meeting a lady friend?'

'Sort of.'

'And what does that mean?'

'It means she's not – she's just a girl I've bumped into.'

'It'd be a real bump, too, your size,' and they cackled together.

'You said you had a job for me.'

She nodded. 'I promised it wouldn't be a brake on other plans. Being up at this hour, you'll have done with it before breakfast.'

He had guessed what the job was and had already gone into the dairy to find the dedication. 'There's a card, but Mr Beardsall hasn't written anything on it.'

'That's no matter.'

'Don't wreaths usually have a message on them?'

'There's not a deal of folks passing through that cemetery, Fergal, and for anyone that does, there's no need for written words.' She halted, her teeth pecking at a lip, the taut ligaments wiring her throat. Finally she conceded, 'But since you consider that's the regular way,

130

then you can put my initials. What difference does it make? I've never pretended they weren't already there.'

He ignored her last sentence; he would reflect on it later. 'There's something else. I don't know what grave to put it on.'

'I'm surprised to hear that. I'd have thought by now you'd have added two and two together. You're not slow, a young man blessed with more than the usual dollop of imagination. Though there are times when I can see you'd be happier without.'

'I don't know which grave,' he persisted.

'Toby Wheatley did what was fitting. We held the service after.'

'Yes.' He waited.

'And still it doesn't click? But then, I recall his name wasn't in the report Gilbert Beardsall gave you. No matter. You've read it elsewhere. On the drawing I kept under the wheelchair's cushion.'

Matthew Bennet. Civil engineer and meticulous draughtsman.

As Fergal tied the wreath to the handle bars of the cycle, he thought: Why can't she pronounce his name?

Then: Why did he drown?

He wished he had not asked himself that question; it bothered him, stuck to him like a burr as he rode down the track but on the road through the village it left him. A radio lilted music through an open window; two dogs loped after him in a brief bid for company; the morning sun did not burn but kept him pleasantly warm. Passing the gate and the hawthorn where Gyp and he had found

Alex, he did not think of her saying, 'I wouldn't live anywhere near this lot,' but he remembered her thanking him for the blanket and her unhesitating: 'There's no suppose about it. If the boy had been swept away you'd have jumped in, same as me.'

He had taken this route because he had promised her that he would look out for the Donkey Lane bridge and at the dam he stopped, uncased the binoculars his father had brought. They were stiff but eventually he had them in focus and scrutinised the water. It was clear that its level had gone down, for along the borders there was a fresh band of silt, the colour of storm clouds; but, looking at the centre, he had no way of calculating the depth. Not a welcoming drop, he thought and gripped the binoculars tightly. They showed him that further up the reservoir the smoothness of the water was speckled; there were islets emerging and slim prongs of gravel, new perches for gulls. But though the glasses were efficient and he refocused for the greater distance, he was not certain of details at the farther end. However, he thought he could locate the spot where on Thursday the water had dimpled round something submerged, and there appeared to be two humps, probably of stone. He decided he would examine them at a closer range when he had dealt with the wreath.

Leaving the dam, Fergal forced the bicycle up the valley slope, cruised through the trees, turned into the wider road and finally found the lane by which Mr Beardsall had returned from Niddford. Not far along it, rearing above the parched meadows, was the solitary cross. Opening into the field which led to it was a gate of wrought iron which he decided must have been moved from Linden church yard. He dropped the cycle on the grass and untied the wreath. Still crouched he saw, through the gate's tracery of leaves and scrolls, a young woman walking along the cemetery path. Her head was bent and she was wearing a long, flowing skirt; but she was unmistakably Alex. He placed the wreath by the side of the gate and called, 'Hi!'

At the sound of his voice she looked up, faltered, then came on. About to say: You're out early; to ask why she was there, how she had done in the exams, he was stopped by her face. He exclaimed, 'Alex, what's the matter?'

She shook her head, unable to risk words. Her nose was raw and swollen; her eyes bloodshot. Fergal noticed that her shoes were soaked with the dew; at her knees, her skirt was damp where she had knelt.

'Come on,' he encouraged, and guided her through the gate.

'Can't stay,' she mumbled.

'Won't you wait a minute?' But she stepped on to the lane. 'Where are you going?'

'To the barn.' Her strength had been sapped by the tears; she stumbled, walking like one tranced.

'Could you ride the bike?'

She nodded.

So he ran back, pushed it to her, gathered up her skirt and held the crossbar while she settled on to the seat. 'I'll be with you, fast as I can. Take care.' He watched until a dip in the road sucked her out of sight.

Quickly he snatched the wreath and raced across the

field, but he could not keep up the pace. The path had been made by mourners and at its end was the massive cross. Fergal slowed down and regarded this lonely field-cemetery.

It was a small rectangle of land fenced off. Its grass, coarse and wild, had neither been cropped by cows nor put to the scythe. At a first glance it appeared empty, but away in a far corner was a cluster of weathered slabs. Headstones. He walked towards them. There were not many, and under them the earth was level and tussocky, not raised in smooth mounds. They were not separated but were crammed close as if, removed from the sheltering walls of Linden, they had been huddled together for comfort in this bleak, wider space. Above them, the fence was capped with barbed wire and he thought: Is that to keep people out or these ones in?

On the graves there were vases. Most lolled empty, furred green where the water had dried out; some held withered flowers. But on a grave that lay apart from the rest a vase had been washed recently. Its glass glinted in the sun, and cascading from its slim neck were red campions and poppies, fresh and brilliant, and cranesbill, its blue stolen from the sky. Fergal stopped and read the name on the headstone. Then he bent down and placed the wreath of lilies by the side of the newly-gathered flowers.

He turned away and left the cemetery. Striding swiftly, mechanically, he did not notice the road or Crashing Beck Lane or the path through the woods. What he saw was Alex's grieving face and on a grave the grass flattened, the froth of dew vanished, soaked up by a pressing skirt.

At the barn the cycle was outside, propped against the wall. Inside, he blinked into the shadows, found her hunched on the straw. Now he was with her he did not know how to speak to her. Consolation was needed, but why should she weep for Matthew Bennet who had died probably before she was born?

'I was sent with a wreath to put on his grave,' he told her. 'I saw your flowers.'

'Who sent you?'

'Mrs Helliwell.'

She blenched. 'Hypocrite.'

'Why do you say that?'

'Because she's pretending to be sorry.'

She was wrong in both of her accusations, but this was not the moment to argue about Mrs Helliwell. 'It was his drawing – Matthew Bennet's – that I told you I'd seen.'

'Yes, I suppose he must have taken several copies.'

'I know that he drowned, but I don't know how it happened.'

'It was at Donkey Lane bridge.'

'Was it? I haven't heard that.'

'Of course you haven't. Nobody talks.' She rubbed her hand over her nose and looked past him, through the door. 'They buried him and that's where they want him to stay. They'd like to believe he never existed. But he did, and they were luckier than me. They knew him. I didn't.' She caught her breath; the tears spurted. 'You see, Fergal, he was my father.'

Fourteen

'He was my father,' Alex repeated. 'He was drowned six months before I was born.'

Fergal had known only one person who had died and that was Grandfather Collins. He remembered him as a giant of a man with whiskers who gave him piggyback rides up to bed.

But he had knelt on the bank by the side of Bailey while the man pounded his chest and there, in the barn, he relived those terrible minutes. His sight clouded, his body grew torpid, his mind swelled with the ache of a failure he could not forgive.

'Please don't take on so,' he begged her and found that he was sitting on the straw, a hand over hers.

'It's seeing where they put him.'

'Yes.'

'Separate from the others.'

He could not deny it.

'Mother was too ill to go.'

For a time they were silent.

She continued, 'I haven't been able to face having a look until now. Perhaps I shouldn't have today, either.' Another sob jerked her.

'They had a service for him in the church. After they had drained the reservoir to demolish it. The spire had shown first time it was filled up. So they held a service.' He was trying to find something to console her.

'Mrs Helliwell wrote and told Mother.'

'I'd expect her to. Him dying hit her hard.' It was more than that, however. You can put my initials on it, the old woman had said about the wreath; I've never pretended they weren't already there. What did she mean?

'That's what Mrs Helliwell made out.' Alex referred to his last remark. 'It wasn't likely she'd say anything else, was it?' She paused, controlling the pumping breaths. 'The reservoir was the first really big thing that Dad worked on. He was excited about it, until he learnt what it entailed.'

To submerge Linden.

'He hated the idea of that, but he hadn't designed the reservoir. There was nothing he could do to stop it.'

'They had a go. Mrs Helliwell told my mother. They blocked the roads. And other things.' None of this was important compared with her father's death, but he wanted to distract her from crying.

She echoed, 'Other things. Yes. They made Dad's life hell.'

'What?'

'He was very junior. Perhaps that was why liaising with the Linden people was passed on to him. He had to explain about the construction to them and tell them the dates they had to move out. So he was the first in the line of fire, as he put it.'

Fergal recalled Desmond Singleton's: They shovelled us out of our homes; and Gilbert Beardsall's bitter comment on the graves: What was in them couldn't be left under water. Not hygienic.

He said, 'It sounds like your father was given a rotten job.'

'Yeh. Everything the people thought about the reservoir and the water authority they took out on him.'

'Why? I don't see.'

'Being as awkward as they could, not co-operating. They ganged up on him, refused their consent, wouldn't sign forms. Everything they could think of, to delay. Normally I expect Dad could have dealt with the hassle, but it was so personal, like saying he enjoyed rehousing them, and that if he honestly disagreed with the policy on Linden, he'd resign. They made him the scapegoat for the water board's decision.'

He did not believe it. Sharp, he demanded, 'How do you know?'

She was not put out by the question. 'I'm sorry, but it's true. I've read Dad's letters. He had to live away from home while he was working here. They loathed him, Fergal.'

He could not answer.

'I shouldn't have gone into it. You happened along at a bad moment.'

'It doesn't matter,' he lied.

'I might have told you on Thursday when we were talking about the bridge but you had said you were staying with Mrs Helliwell, and that put me off.'

139

He wanted to say: I like Mrs Helliwell; she wouldn't be spiteful. But he could not argue. Alex's tears were not dry and through his mind were tolling the lines Agnes Greaves Helliwell had written on the map:

Because I fear God
I will not curse them.
But I cannot forget
Or forgive.

He saw that his hand still lay over Alex's and he withdrew it.

'Yes,' she acknowledged the movement. 'Time to get on.'

'What with?'

'Well, I can't claim I've got a backlog of engagements.' Her expression lightened. 'Some time today I'll have to buy food, though. Damn, I forgot. It's Sunday. Will there be a shop open in Niddford?'

'I've no idea.'

'It's irrelevant anyway. There isn't a bus. But it doesn't matter; I've got some biscuits. Then I have to see if Donkey Lane bridge is showing yet.'

'It might be.'

'Might be?'

'I thought I could make out something this morning, but I was on the dam. Too far to be sure, even with binoculars.'

'But you saw something,' she insisted. 'That's ace. As soon as I read in the papers that this reservoir was getting so low, I knew I had to come because probably it would

140

go down as far as that bridge. It could be the only chance I'll ever have to see exactly where it happened.'

'Alex, you mustn't . . .'

'I've got one or two of his belongings,' she interrupted, 'his drawings, his favourite hat, but they aren't enough. This is where he worked and for these last three weeks I've been where he was, where he walked. Then suddenly it all ended for him. And if I can see where it ended, I might be able to let him rest. I might not feel so bad.'

The intensity of her speech alarmed him. 'Look, Alex, leave it for an hour or two, will you? I don't know what time you left home to get to the cemetery so early . . . '

'I travelled overnight, got a taxi from the coach station.'

'So you need to eat. I'll fetch you something.'

'I've got biscuits.'

'You can't live on those. I'll fetch some stuff. You'll wait till I get back?'

'I'll wait. As a matter of fact, I am feeling peckish.'

When he arrived at the farmhouse, Madge was preparing breakfast. 'I'm late this morning,' she greeted. 'Had a marvellous night's sleep, then Philip rang.' From a distance of sixty centimetres she lobbed a tea bag towards the pot and missed. Retrieving it, Fergal admonished silently: Be your age, Mother. Getting high on a phone call! Aloud, he said, 'Don't bother about breakfast for me.'

'Agnes told me you were about early, taking the wreath to the cemetery, but I didn't realise you'd got your own breakfast.' She glanced at the table for evidence, located the jar of marmalade and jug of milk that she herself had just placed there, then took a carton of yoghurt out of the refrigerator, examined it curiously and replaced it.

'You can count me out for lunch as well, Mother.' It was not worth correcting her mistake about the breakfast. 'I'm going to pack myself something; don't know when I'll be in.'

'As you wish, Fergal,' she murmured serenely. It was possible that she had not heard.

With Madge in this mood, he could collect together double rations without offering reasons. He fetched his rucksack and stocked up. But as he drew water from the tap to make cordial, he had to claim her attention. 'Is Mr Beardsall filling the tank again today?'

'What?' She thought over his question. 'Ah, the water. He said he'd collect the drums. He didn't want them on his truck last night.'

'What about delivery?'

'I hope this evening.'

'I used to pump up twice a day. Remember?'

'Yes, and it was good of you to do it.'

'Mother! The point is, if he's coming once a day, then we have to use half as much.'

'I can do my sums, Fergal, thank you,' she told him, huffy; then, as he was going: 'By the amount of food you're taking, I can only say it's lucky we don't have to halve what you eat.'

That showed you could never be certain that she had not noticed.

In the barn he found Alex asleep. She lay with her face crushed into his pillow and her skirt was rucked up her legs. He could see that the rash on her calves was less fiery and he was glad that he had brought her the blanket.

Squatting on the floor, he opened the bottle of cordial and took a long swig. The breeze that had flicked his curtain several hours earlier had passed and the heat had swept back, its strength restored. But it was not dry now, taut and refined to steel; it was sticky and flaccid, a smothering pelt. Though the stone wall of the barn was cold, leaning against it Fergal could feel the sweat slide down his spine.

It was the first thing that Alex remarked on when she woke. 'Hi, there! Heavens, it feels like thunder.'

Without thinking, he answered, 'I'd be glad of a spot of rain.'

'Not me.'

So he assured her, 'It'll take a long time for the reservoir to fill up.'

'If that bridge is the last thing to show, it'll be the first to be covered again.'

'I expect so. I'd never set eyes on a reservoir till now.'

'Same here.'

He thought that she might jump up that minute and race towards Linden. 'Have breakfast first.'

Eating, she told him about her examination results and without the usual embarrassment he was able to say, 'I don't take A levels for another three years.'

'Why's that? Have you had a gap or something?'

'Like what? Being detained at Her Majesty's pleasure?'

He was glad of her smile. 'No, I haven't. Had a gap.'

'You do surprise me.'

'By the time I was thirteen visitors to school took me for a member of staff.'

'I wasn't referring to *size*.'

Her answer, not his confession, made him blush.

It was past midday before they finished their meal. Alex told him, 'Do you know, I've been getting through a dishful of food at a rate of knots. When you're alone, you don't really enjoy eating, it's to stoke up. Sometimes I've thought I'd go batty, talking to myself.'

'I suppose that's a hazard.'

Amused, she teased, 'You're right there, Grandpa.'

Gathering together what food remained, she began to pack it into Fergal's rucksack. 'You can keep it,' he told her.

'I was hoping you'd say that. Thanks. It's all so delicious. These pasties! But I was putting it out of the way so that nothing would get at it, though I don't know what.'

'Sheep are veggies. Different from wolves.'

Her eyes opened, then she laughed. 'Point to you. Now, what did I mean to do before we go out?' she asked herself.

She was expecting him to go with her. Feeling his chest and shoulders relax, Fergal realised he had been anxious that she might decline his company.

'I know. I want to change into my shorts.' She took the shorts out of her bag and thrust her feet into them. Fergal was uncertain whether he should go outside while

144

she did this, but to remain seemed more cool, so he compromised. Keeping his eyes turned from her, he buckled up the rucksack and placed it in a corner of the barn.

'That's it,' she announced, and tossed away the skirt. She had dressed under it. 'Ready when you are.'

Fifteen

Leaving the barn, they strode across the meadow and climbed through the gully. Its steep cleft and the jumbled rocks on its bed were the only signs that a gill had once flowed there.

'The spring for the farm's dried up, too,' Fergal told her and explained how the house was supplied.

'I bet Dad would have been interested in that.'

'Do you know if he ever went to the farm after everyone had been moved out of Linden?'

'There's no mention of it in any of his letters.'

They skirted the plantation behind the farm, crossed the track and took Mrs Helliwell's path through the woods on the other side.

Alex said, 'If it didn't mean the water's going down, I'd be sick of this heat. It isn't any cooler out of the sun. Couldn't you kill a shower?'

'I'd feel just as hot five minutes after.'

'A swim, then.'

'I suppose.' It was two months since he had been to his local baths. 'You can lose interest.'

'In what?'

'Swimming.'

'Have you?'

'At the moment.'

'Any reason?'

'I've got a block.' She waited for him to explain. 'Something went wrong. Not at the swimming baths. I was with a friend.'

Watching his face, she asked tentatively, 'Did something happen to him?'

'Yes.'

'I'm sorry, Fergal. That must have been terrible,' Her face had twisted; she had concluded that, like her father, Bailey had drowned.

Hastily he assured her, 'He was all right, a man got him out. I couldn't. I was . . .' He could not speak of it.

'You're blaming yourself, aren't you?'

He nodded. Eventually, he managed: 'It's not as if I'm a poor swimmer, and I'm as good under water as I am on top.'

'I'm sure.'

'I let him down. I'm no good.'

'Yes, you are!' She was suddenly fierce. 'It's bad, talking like that about yourself.'

He shook his head.

Alex strode ahead of him, then swung round. 'Have it your own way, then. Just stay a rotten, selfish slob who hasn't a moment to give to anyone else and would never think of lending a dosser a blanket and who hasn't the first notion of how to repair a bicycle.'

She was willing him to smile but he answered, 'That's not the same.'

'Do you know what else you are? Obstinate.'

'Nobody's called me that before.'

'What do they call you?'

'Pretty much what you did: a rotten selfish slob . . .'

Then they were laughing. 'Caught you on that one,' he said.

After that, they did not return to the 'incident in the river'. Sensing that Fergal had said all that he could, Alex did not press him to confide any more.

In Linden they found that visitors had left the usual litter. There was chocolate paper in the beck, plastic bottles in a hearth, a can crunched into a tree's roots. Under the church bridge someone had dumped a polystyrene tray.

'I don't like to see this,' she said.

'No.'

'I might even fetch a bag later, collect it all up. Would that be crazy?'

'It'd be a nice sort of crazy.' He commented to himself: She can consider doing that, in spite of hating the neighbourhood and the people. She feels the same way about Linden as I do.

So he told her how he had described the village to his father and Philip's story about the bombed-out house.

'I can understand why the children didn't go back there,' she commented. 'Can you?'

'I'll say. I'd run a mile first.'

'Your father sounds a nice man, Fergal.'

'He's not bad.' Catching her smile, he admitted, 'OK. We get on. Only I shouldn't be talking about him when yours . . . when you haven't . . .'

'You can't pretend you haven't got one because mine is dead. I like hearing about other people's fathers. I build into it how I imagine mine might have been.'

They had come to the end of the houses and were now walking between the fallen walls of Donkey Lane. Ahead of them it was a slender strand reaching into the reservoir. Then it disappeared under the water, emerged and climbed the opposite bank. Roughly in the middle of its hidden route were two wedges of masonry. Not yet fully exposed, they appeared unimportant, squat.

'They're further away than you think,' Fergal said. 'We'll see better with these.' He examined the structure quickly through the binoculars and handed them to Alex.

'It looks odd,' she reported.

'Only because it's a different design from the church bridge.'

'Yeh, and I like that. This one hasn't a parapet or an arch.' She sounded disappointed. 'It's just two heaps of stones.'

'They'll be the piers, like pillars, both sides of the river.' There were four and a half to six metres between them. 'It was a footbridge, wasn't it, according to the map? I expect the span of this would be flat, made of planks.'

'I can't see any.'

'Probably been washed away.'

She fiddled with the wheel of the binoculars, trying to improve the focus. 'I haven't the patience for these. Let's go nearer.'

The lane was compacted earth dusted with sand until, descending steeply, it curved into the water and became a bar of silt.

'This is where we pulled up the other day,' Alex said, pointing to a mess of prints. 'The little boy must have been about here.' It was a good distance from the present edge of the reservoir.

'Your cycle tracks are way back, now.'

'Don't remind me. You must've thought I was brainless.'

'No. Crazy.'

'You don't know the half of it.'

Fergal thought: Save me from that.

He followed her along the rib of Donkey Lane. The water was receding so quickly that the surface had no time to dry out and was moist as a beach between tides. But as they drew closer to the bridge it became wetter, spongy, and water oozed. It filled then obliterated their tracks.

'This is far enough,' Fergal cautioned.

'I can see something else.'

'It could be one of the timbers that ran across connecting the two pillars. They'd support the planks.'

'I want to get closer.'

'No.'

'We can take our shoes off.'

'Alex, it's not a case of getting just our feet wet. The bridge is still a long way from here and we can't estimate the depth at the pillars – we don't know how far they go down. And flowing underneath, between them, is the river.'

'It's not much of one.'

'It's still a river. It seems to spread out when it enters the reservoir, after it drops down those waterfalls, but its course must come straight to this bridge. It'll flow under the surface.'

'I'd be surprised if it had the energy.'

'It's not exactly in spate, I know that, but its banks are steep. Higher up, you can see they aren't completely levelled off. I bet they go deep at the bridge. Mrs Helliwell has mentioned currents.'

'Mrs Helliwell!' she scorned.

'Yeh. She ought to know.'

'OK, you win.' However, before Fergal could congratulate himself on his powers of persuasion, she added, 'I think we could get nearer from the other side. We can walk round this end of the reservoir if we go back up Crashing Beck Lane.'

'I know that. But I reckon the bridge isn't any closer to the other side. You'll have to wait longer, until the water's far enough out for it to be reasonably safe.'

'Fergal, has anyone ever told you that you're bossy?'

'No, but I'm working on it.'

'You're making good progress. Come on, then. I need a kip, preferably long. An overnight coach doesn't rock you to sleep.'

'Shall I come to the barn tomorrow morning?'

'That would be nice.'

'We could go into Niddford, try out the casinos, the amusement arcades, the betting shops, massage parlours. If they aren't open, we could visit Tracie at the launderette.'

'And I could have a wash. I'm not sure though, about tomorrow. It depends on . . .' and she made a gesture towards the bridge behind them.

He tried to reason: 'Alex, you've looked at it. I know you want to see where your father . . . but why be so fixed on getting nearer?'

She stopped, squeezed a shoe into the mud.

'It won't tell you anything,' he persisted.

'I know it's not logical, but I can't get my head round what happened there, Fergal. It nags at me; it won't go away.'

'Do you know whether he could swim?'

'Yes, he could swim.'

The water was rising up her shoe, frothing brown against the welt. And he could see Bailey's mouth, the air bubbling out, his eyes watching Fergal's hands that had become crippled, bent and inflexible, refusing to release the wire, while above it the water curdled with their mingled blood. 'You can get into difficulties,' he told her. 'You never know what might be under the surface, what you might get caught on.'

Half understanding his reference, she shuddered. 'Yes; that's true, and it could have been like that. But why was he in the river at all? I won't believe that he could have,' she winced, 'that he could have thrown himself in. So I ask myself . . .'

Fergal waited.

'I keep asking myself,' she said quietly, 'was Dad pushed?'

'No!' The word burst out, harsh and scared. 'No, it's

not possible. Nobody would do that.'

She looked at him and for a moment her expression was sympathetic, then it hardened. 'Remember, they hated him, Fergal,' she said.

Sixteen

When Fergal returned to the farmhouse he found Madge trilling a syrupy lyric he was glad he didn't know while she stroked an iron gently over a pair of shorts.

'I was thinking I could wear these,' she told him.

'Why not?'

'But at my age?'

He answered silently: Look, Mother, I've more things to worry about. Aloud, he said, 'Up to you.'

'I can't decide.' She dangled them in front of her stomach. 'What's your honest opinion?'

'They'd look better without the apron underneath.'

Surprised, she looked down and he thought: She's as bad as she was this morning. On one phone call from Dad.

'I'll try them on later,' she decided. 'One thing's for sure: Philip likes me in this shade.'

'Does that mean you're seeing him?'

'Of course. Didn't I mention it this morning? He's taking the day off tomorrow.'

'But it's only yesterday he came up!'

'He won't drive both ways. He'll stay overnight.'

Going back to the ironing board, she became

immersed in a floral shirt. However, she did notice when Fergal handed her a cup of tea.

'Lovely!' she thanked him and, seeing him open the oven door, advised: 'You won't find anything in there. From what you took with you after breakfast, I thought you wouldn't need a full meal this evening but there's some salad at the bottom of the fridge and you can always boil an egg.'

Fergal arranged a tomato and some lettuce leaves on a plate and regarded them grimly. When a woman has a date with her husband, what price is the well-being of her son?

It was difficult to think lucidly against Madge's warblings. All that came to him were pictures: of a body dropping from a bridge; of a spout of water that rose up, paused, cascaded down, then subsided and was forever still; of a slim package bearing the words Black Monday; of a wreath of lilies. And he heard a man saying, 'It's not something I'm anxious to look on, but you'll have no trouble with it, being a stranger;' and an old woman asking, 'Do you believe God punishes, Fergal?' and a girl insisting, 'They hated him.'

These pictures and voices were still crowding his mind when he heard Gilbert Beardsall's truck and he did not dash out to help carry in the water. He felt squeamish; he did not wish to meet him. Madge, returned to housekeeping mode, had to prompt him with: 'Mr Beardsall's here, Fergal. I'm sure he'd appreciate a hand.'

Being a man who valued silence, Gilbert Beardsall was not perturbed by Fergal's. His speech was addressed to himself and was confined to grumbles about the weight of the drums. Until, the tank filled and the empty drums stacked in the truck, he exclaimed, 'Carting water's no job for this weather. Never known it so close. Like it's seeing how far it can go before it cracks up.'

'Do you think there'll be rain soon?' Madge asked him.

'I'm no weather prophet, but it can't go on like this much longer. Something's got to give. I'm amazed you can stand there and take the heat coming off that iron, Mrs Collins, an evening like this.'

'I'm having a holiday tomorrow.'

'And not before time. Do you want me to call in, do the necessary for Mrs Helliwell?'

'Thank you, but Fergal will be here.'

'That's so.' He saw Fergal's resentment that his presence should be taken for granted and, winking at him, promised quietly, 'We'll see.'

After he had paid his 'respects to the old lady' and gone, Madge asked, 'Would you mind taking Agnes the orange juice I've made for her; it's in the fridge.'

He gave the first excuse that occurred to him. 'I'm taking Gyp for a walk.'

At the word, the dog rolled her eyes and attempted an obedient interest.

'She's not keen,' Madge translated. 'She knows where it's cooler.'

'You'll soon brighten up, won't you Gyp?'

She gave a token flick of her tail then padded to her bowl and drank greedily.

So, out-manouevred, Fergal carried the orange juice in

to Mrs Helliwell's room. She was covered not by a sheet but by a large square of muslin that was creamy and loose woven. Under it, her body was narrow, the legs mere bone, skewed at the joints.

He put the glass on the table beside her but she did not glance at it, keeping her eyes on his face. She had slipped off the supporting pillows and he bent down, righted them, remembering how that morning she had allowed him to lift her. It seemed like another day. He had been saddened by her blush. Now the colour of her face did not alter from its chalky white.

Without preamble, she began, 'You saw there were flowers put for him.'

He nodded.

'Flowers of the meadows, wild things, not a stiff wreath. Natural, not forced.'

He did not answer.

'And you've been with her all day, the girl.'

Again he nodded. The time for evasion was past.

'It was known she was hereabouts. She kept tight to herself. Things were done and not seen. Such as the rosemary.' For a second she halted. 'That frighted me, Fergal. Worse than a ghost.'

He wondered whether from the beginning she had suspected in whose memory it had been left.

'You've talked to her. Why does she stay?' She was pleading with him to speak.

'She's waiting for the reservoir to go down more. She wants to get to Donkey Lane bridge.'

'Why's that? Tell me.'

'You can guess.' He was torturing her for Alex's sake.

'You can be hard, Fergal, as it turns out. I'd never have thought it. Donkey Lane bridge is nothing to her, such a young one. What happened there is a matter for us that are left.'

'What did happen there?'

Her shoulders jerked. She snapped, 'That's no business of yours.'

'You haven't said that about anything else, not when you've wanted me to find something out, fetch news, do a job.' Was it really him speaking like this?

She accepted his criticism. 'I've asked more than was fit. You've a right to call me to account. Who's to know what happened at the bridge? I can only say what went on before.'

'She's told me a bit about that.'

'As if she had the knowledge.' For a moment scorn gleamed across her face.

'She's read some of Matthew Bennet's letters.' Deliberately emphasising each word he told her, 'He was her father.'

'No!' The muslin on the bed was clamped between her clenched legs. 'She's telling stories, a regular mischief maker. He had no children.'

'Not when he died. Alex was born afterwards. You should know that. You wrote to his wife.'

Agnes Helliwell's eyes closed; her mouth worked. 'She never answered. I think you'd best go now, Fergal. Let me be.'

He thought: That's right, get rid of me as soon as I'm

no more use. Then he heard her murmur, 'Meadow flowers, cranesbill and campions. Poppies meant to console. Did they give her consolation?'

And he hissed at her, 'No, they didn't. I'd be surprised if anything could. Alex won't rest till she's been on that bridge and seen where her father fell.' He paused. 'Or was pushed.'

Her eyes opened. For the first time he saw that they were the same colour as Alex's but without the gold flecks. Through the horror at what he had just said, he watched the lids quiver, then pinch.

Finally she answered, 'Pushed? Is that what she imagines? I'm sorry to hear you repeat it. That young woman has poisoned your thoughts.'

He walked out of the house and stood in the yard, his breath coming in pants. He felt as if he had done something brutal, bullied a first former, beaten up a beggar, whipped a dog cringing on its leash. Sickened, he held up his hands, spread out the fingers, examined them closely. The nail of one was broken, but they were moderately clean. Across the right palm a line wormed from the little finger to the wrist. Polished white, it was puckered a little where the wire had fastened before slicing down. He said to himself: I tried to free him, but . . . The scar was no comfort. He lowered his hands. They had been useless. Next time, he must do better. Whatever his thoughts meant by that. But it was not some time in the future, a next time. It was this time. Now.

For they both needed him. Mrs Helliwell and Alex. Yet if he were loyal to one, he could not avoid hurting the other. He saw the pain in the old woman's face as she answered, 'Pushed?' It could not be true. It was not possible.

By the side of her face was another's. Alex's. It, too, was appalled. Looking at it, Fergal longed for something simple. He wanted to put his own face against it, feel her lips.

The heat had soaked up the air; there was none left for breathing. He would go to Alex, try to make her understand that Mrs Helliwell could not have done it or ordered it to be done.

Though she had spoken of punishment.

Slowly he walked out of the yard and tramped through the plantation. Far in the distance was a low ponderous sound. He stopped and listened. Round him the trees were like stone, stiff columns waiting. The birds were silent. The sound continued, a great cumbersome weight trundling. Thunder.

For the second time that day, Alex was asleep when he came to the barn. Her face was turned to the door and her expression was serene. Briefly he debated whether to rouse her but decided to leave her a note. Talk would be easier after they had both slept. Usually he did not carry a pen, but that morning he had pocketed one after putting Mrs Helliwell's name on the wreath, and in the rucksack he had left were bread rolls in a paper bag. He tore off a scrap of it and wrote: I'll be with you early as I can. Please don't do anything before that. There's something I want to talk about. Fergal. Finding her trainers, he threaded the paper under a lace.

161

This done, he looked back at Alex. She had pushed a hand under her cheek and as breath suddenly wheezed out, a few bubbles gathered and slid on to her chin. He felt that he should not have seen that, it was so intimate and made her seem vulnerable and like a child. Not the young woman who had taken these paths alone through the smothering woods. He wished he could lie down beside her, squeeze her tight against his chest. Bailey had mentioned frolicking in the hay. That, too, Fergal thought, and his blood raced.

Trudging home, he heard again the thunder. Although it growled, circling the valley, it did not advance, compressing its power. But, on entering the yard, he saw a few drops of rain. They hit the ground, spread darkly then immediately faded, dried by the cement's heat. Some fell on his head and sieved through his hair. Gratefully he let them drip down his neck.

At the door, his mother said, 'I was beginning to think this would never come. Surely when it gets going it won't be so hot? I'm trying to persuade Agnes to take a sleeping draught; she's overwrought with this weather.'

As usual, he thought, her diagnosis is wrong.

She told him, 'It's a pity you've been out. There was a phone call from Bailey.'

'No!'

'Why shouldn't he ring? Especially when you haven't answered his letter.'

'I haven't got round to it.'

'I said you'd been very busy.'

'Thanks.'

'I don't know why I told him that. You could easily have found time to write.'

'Did he say anything?'

'Not a great deal. He's very sparing with his speech, isn't he? Though I've heard him going sixty to the dozen with you.'

'I meant, did he happen to mention why he was phoning?'

'He wanted to know when we're leaving here. He seemed anxious to see you.'

Fergal sighed to himself: Wish I could say the same, Bailey, but nothing's changed. I shan't feel any different when I get back.

Before returning to the kitchen, Madge said, 'I'd like you to take down that clothes line.'

'Why?'

'With all this electricity about.' She gestured up to the sky. Obligingly, a patch of it gleamed with lightning. 'See?'

'But that can't do any harm to a length of rope. The stuff that conducts is . . .'

'Please, Fergal,' she interrupted.

So he fetched the ladder and unhitched the rope. Taking it into the dairy, he could hardly see the lumber through the twilight of the imminent storm. The first time he had visited Linden he had borrowed Wellington boots; this evening he rejected them and groped until his hand identified waders. There were two pairs; he tried them on and chose the pair that was the better fit.

He did not ask himself why he did this. He did not

wish to acknowledge the premonition that caused him to stand the waders by the dairy door. As he coiled up the rope and placed it beside them, he recited a list of formulae, hummed a favourite track. Tricks to repulse painful dreams or to prevent his mind from lingering on alarming subjects. Such as rain, and a river, and a young woman's obsession with Donkey Lane bridge.

Seventeen

The drops of rain were a warning – or a promise – of what was to come. No more fell that evening, as if it could not spill out until the lightning and thunder had spent their power, had singed and drummed.

Throughout the night they darted and wheeled over the head of the valley. At times they came closer and the rooms in the farmhouse were lit by brief, blinding flares, the windows shook and the water in the reservoir was dyed scarlet with the sky's spurting flames. Once a shaft found Linden, bleached its ruins like bones picked over, then outstripping the thunder, it sprang across the river and ran up the slopes until it found the deserted cemetery. There it slithered along the gate, rose up the huge cross, scorched the wreath of lilies and glimmered, iridescent, on the vase which held the frail meadow flowers.

But still there was no rain.

Fergal could not sleep. Sweat puddled his skin. Although the window was open, the room was so airless he thought he would choke. Hoping to create a draught, he got up and unlatched the door. In the pause before the imminent cannon of thunder, he heard murmurs, a step across the passage and the clink of cups: his mother brewing tea for herself and Mrs Helliwell. He returned to his bed, pulled off the sheet and stretched out naked in the path of the draught.

He was not aware that he slept. He believed that he spent the night listening to the explosions of thunder while the lightning patterned the ceiling and walls. Yet the sound of a car and Gyp's bark roused him. Groping for his watch, he forced his eyes to open and had to concede that it was nine o'clock. Slowly, clumsily, he dressed and, searching for a shirt, realised that it was not fully daylight; the sky was dark as charcoal, without sun or stars. As he walked down the stairs he heard the thunder-tumbrils lumber down the valley, clanking, unsatisfied.

'We must stop meeting like this,' his father greeted him.

Fergal groaned. Another one that was high.

Philip was wearing a sand-coloured linen suit. In his hand was a large bunch of flowers. 'For the women,' he explained.

'I'd be worried if they were for me.'

'I could spare you a button-hole.'

'It would look better with your gear.'

'Do you like it?'

'It's an improvement on Mother's shorts.'

'Have I ever worn those? Must have been drunk.'

'Dad, do you mind? I've only just got up.'

'Still keeping to the old habits? I was up before dawn,' Philip told him, smug, then he gestured grandly to the table. 'Try some breakfast. Madge has had hers.

She's attending to Mrs Helliwell.'

Later when Madge joined them, she said, 'Well, that's Agnes ready for the day. It took longer than usual to get her dressed.'

Philip asked, 'How is she?'

'Considering the broken night, she's surprisingly full of beans.'

'Wish I was,' Fergal muttered.

'In fact, I get the impression that she's excited, which seems a bit odd, almost as if she's feverish, but her temperature's normal. She's very keen for us to have a good day but I think she's really saying that she wants to get rid of us.'

Fergal said to himself: I know how she feels; I wish they'd *go*.

'She says she has business with you, Fergal.'

'What business?' His stomach twisted.

'I've no idea.'

'Well, it'd better not take long. I'm doing something.'

'Surely you don't intend to take that poor dog for a walk again? Not while it's like this.'

'No.'

Philip asked tentatively, 'Fixed up all day?'

'Maybe.'

Disappointed, his parents regarded each other, their eyes asking questions. Madge began, 'In that case, I don't think we ought . . .'

'Oh, for heaven's sake clear out, the pair of you,' Fergal snapped. 'I shan't be far away. I'll nip back to check that she's all right.'

'That's good of you.'

Dependable Fergal.

After that, they were not long leaving. Philip went to introduce himself to Mrs Helliwell and Madge collected an umbrella: 'The rain can't hold off much longer.' Then they were in the car and crunching down the track. As the sound faded, it was replaced by the jingle of the bell in the old woman's room.

As usual she was sitting propped up by pillows but everything else about her had changed. She was not wearing a cardigan or bed jacket nor was the rest of her covered by a sheet. That had been discarded and a white bedspread trimmed with lace had been placed under her. Against it, the purple and wines in her dress smouldered and her legs were profiled, black-stockinged, thick at the ankles but with neat calves. The cuffs of the long sleeves were fastened with gilt buttons and a long line of them stretched down the centre of the dress from throat to hem. Her hair had been brushed from its plaits and hung crinkled over her shoulders and there was a hint of colour in her cheeks, deepening the fierce eyes.

'I let Madge think I was prettifying for your father,' she answered Fergal's amazement, 'but he isn't the visitor I have in mind. Though he's a proper man, I'll say that, and thoughtful. He's left me his telephone for use should there be need. Never wanted one of them, though Martin would fuss. When I always had Gyp!'

'Mother said you had business for me.'

'I'm calling on you to spare me some time, in spite of

what was said last night. You'll be seeing that daughter of his?'

'Yes.'

'That's as I expected. So when we've finished what there is to be done, I want you to fetch her here.'

Astounded, he told her, 'I can't do that.'

'You must use your tongue artfully. Persuade her.'

'She won't come.'

'I have to speak to her, Fergal. I can't go through any more nights like the last. That poison of hers has to be purged.'

'It's not poison. She's just trying to work it out. Her father could swim, and anyway why was he in the river? That's why she wonders if he was pushed.' He thought: Are we having this conversation or am I dreaming it?

'He wasn't pushed, Fergal, not in the way she imagines.'

'What do you mean?'

'There are other ways of pushing than striking a hand in the small of the back and I want to tell her. I must be the one. Will you say that?'

He nodded.

'Champion. Now, there's something I have to look on before the rain comes. I turned my eyes from it when we went to the church, gave him a memorial, but that didn't spare me. It's stayed in my sight this last eighteen years. I couldn't put it from me.'

'What's that?'

She tutted. 'Are you addle-brained this morning? She's come to the place of it, she whose father was drowned there, and I must see it, too. I'm not seeking a cure but when I speak to her I want to know I've had the courage to do what she's done.'

She was asking him to take her to Donkey Lane bridge. 'No,' he objected. 'I can't get you there.'

'Don't fuss yourself. Were you thinking I was set on a joy ride in the wheelchair, or on the crossbar of that bike?' She gave a sudden cackle. 'Mind you, it'd be a romp, trying it, but we have to pay heed to sense. You get me to my old room. I can see from the skylight.'

Before that there were two flights of stairs. 'I don't think Mother would . . .'

'I'll take responsibility,' she interrupted him. 'It's my life and limb. Such as they are. You'll help me? But don't think I'm trying to coax you with this.' She looked down at her body. 'I loathe it too much to ask sympathy for what it won't let me do. You say you will or you won't, and that's the end of it.'

'How much do you weigh?'

Agnes smiled and scratched a stiff claw on her thigh. 'That's more like it. You can save yourself a bit of toil if you wheel me to the bottom of the stairs. Hasn't Madge put the chair by the front door against me sitting in the garden again?'

Fetching it, Fergal looked at his watch. The time was fifteen minutes past ten. He debated: Shall I rush out to the barn first, explain to Alex that Mrs Helliwell can tell her how her father died, ask her not to go any nearer the place where it happened? But the old woman waited for him in her room and her wheel-chair was under his hand.

'I'll be with you soon, Alex,' he said aloud. 'Wait for me. Don't do anything reckless. Don't do another Bailey on me. Promise me that.'

As he pushed the chair down the passage, the first lightning of the day snapped on. For a second the sky was gilded, then it returned to its former grey.

Eighteen

Fergal stood the chair by a wall, pushed the rug against the wheels to prevent them rolling, then lifted Mrs Helliwell from the bed and eased her into the seat.

'See, a piece of cake,' she congratulated. 'With those muscles on you, you could pick up two of me and not notice.' Her bent fingers kept up a continual scratching at the pattern of her dress, a sign of the nervous excitement that was to see her through her purpose.

At the bottom of the stairs he took her out of the chair then carried her up the first flight. Her weight was no difficulty but he had to hold her at a sideways angle and make sure that his heels did not project over the stairs' narrow treads.

'You're as good as my Edward, acting porter,' she told him. 'I had to have my bed brought down after he had gone. Our Martin never mastered the knack.' But she winced as Fergal swayed and one of her feet hit the banister rail.

'This isn't the best way to carry you.' He was bearing her like a ceremonial garment across his arms. 'We ought to try a fireman's lift.'

'I don't fancy the sound of that.'

'It would be safer.' But at the head of the stairs he did not stop. He was not sure that he wanted her slung over his shoulder, her legs pinned against his chest. However, an accident decided it.

He continued to the end of the landing and pushed the chenille curtain aside. Immediately they were at the staircase, a steep, narrow shaft. There was a pane of glass in the roof but the slate sky offered no light. His vision constricted, Fergal stepped forward, his foot unexpectedly tripped and he was thrown against the wall. The impact jolted the old woman but as he recovered his balance all she said was: 'I'm grateful you kept hold.' Not until later did he remember that she had not cried out.

Shuffling to examine the floor under them, he explained, 'There's a slit in the lino. A bit's sticking up.'

'I've told Martin about that more than once. It'll have to be that fireman's lift, then, so's you can see what's what.'

In his bedroom he sat her on the chest of drawers. 'I want to start from standing up.'

'You're the expert.'

'I wish I was. Can you hang on for a minute?' Unsupported, she slumped. 'One of my laces is broken.'

'Best see to it. We don't want any more mishaps.'

While he pulled the lace out of the shoe and knotted the pieces together, Agnes told him, 'That lino's no different to the rest of the house it's laid in. Neglected, or half done. Martin was never a one to stir himself unless pushed and his father bequeathed no example. In this house, that is. Not that I blame Edward. His soul was in

Linden and when that went under the water he was left no more than a husk.

'You see, he'd persuaded himself it could never happen. He refused to believe that they could flood the valley. "Not all this good farming land," he'd say. He wouldn't listen. He took no heed of the plans. Even when we were moved into this house, he pretended it could never be. "This is a precaution," he'd declare. "What they have in mind isn't much bigger than a dew pond in the valley bottom." He'd say that though he could see the work going on.

'It was then he did up the room in the attic for me, and a good job he made of it, too. "That skylight'll give you plenty of sun for your pictures, Agnes," he'd say; he was proud of my paintings. "And when you open it and look out of a morning you'll get a fine view of the river and the spire of the church."

'Then they closed the dam and the water built up. Edward went down and watched it rise over the forge that had been his great grandfather's, the one who was killed shoeing horses in the Crimean War. After the rest of the village was covered, its name never passed his lips. He left his farrier's tools in the attic and he used the dairy as a dump for the rest. The ones he'd bought because, "I'm going to beautify this place for you, Agnes." That's what he had said.'

To spare her from his eyes, Fergal made a show of adjusting the lace and drawing it tight.

Her voice firmer, she said, 'Well, that's enough about my Edward.'

'I hadn't worked it out. Not like that.'

'I'd not expect it.' She paused. 'It's long years past. And do you know, I've got that sometimes I can say to myself: They need the water, those forced to dwell in towns.' She started as lightning sliced into the room, followed by the thump of thunder. 'That was close! Now I warn you I've no head for heights,' and she tried to smile as he prepared to pick her up.

Afterwards, Fergal regretted hauling her on to his shoulder although it made his task easier. For Agnes, folded over, the position pulled at her cramped joints and her crusty spine twitched and throbbed. When they entered the room and he laid her on the sofa, he saw that the brief journey had scored the pain lines deeper into her face.

'Shall I get you something?' he asked her.

'This isn't the time for pampering.' Then as the room was stabbed by light and shaken by thunder, she muttered, 'It's the day for seeing.'

He glanced at the skylight above them. How were they to manage? 'I could come after you've had a rest.'

'I don't need a rest, not the sort you're meaning. It's memories I want a rest from, but they'll not allow. In all the time since the flooding that skylight's not been opened. Edward wasn't the only one that didn't wish to see that there wasn't a view of the river any longer, or the spire of the church. I'd sit with my pictures,' she looked round at the studies of Linden, 'but they didn't give any comfort. Because along with these places that lay under the water, there was another, and no picture could

176

quieten the knowledge of that.' Her face was pallid but her mouth was stern. 'So now will you be good enough to open the skylight, Fergal? Black Monday's the last day I looked on Donkey Lane bridge, little knowing what the night would bring. But I'll look on today. To my shame, it's needed his daughter's prompting.'

And I'll be with her soon, Fergal told himself. He climbed on to a chair, released the latch of the skylight, pushed the frame up and fixed it open at the last hole in the rod. The height provided a view that was not suspected on the other floors of the house. The meadows at the front hid the nearer slopes of the valley but the opposite side of the reservoir was visible and the water at its base. At a sharp angle to his left he could make out the blunt piers of Donkey Lane bridge but he did not pause to scrutinise them.

'I can hold you up to it,' he said, although that meant he had to support her almost at the full stretch of his arms; he could not lift her and at the same time mount the chair. 'But you'll have to try to hang on to the frame.'

She regarded her knotted fingers and hissed at them, disgusted, 'You'll have to shape up.'

He helped her into a sitting position, grasped her at the waist and carried her towards the skylight. 'Dig your feet into my sides,' he instructed, but without guidance she could not do it and her legs were left dangling. The strain on her spine trembled through her and entered his hands. In a lurch that nearly brought him over, she drove a shoulder against the frame, held it there and looked out.

'Can you see?' he asked.

'As much as I want. It's as bare as a baby's bottom, not what it was before, nor what they made of it after. It's a blessing Crashing Beck bank hides the village, where it was. Donkey Lane bridge is standing out.' She was suddenly profiled by lightning. He heard a gasp and a low exclamation before thunder rattled the skylight and shuddered the walls.

'I don't think you ought to stay any longer.'

'Wait.'

He could feel that her body had clenched; her legs had stiffened; the veins worming round her ankles bulged through the stockings. She had grown heavier, spreading an ache along his arms. At last he disturbed her silence. 'I'll have to bring you down.'

Above him, her head nodded.

As he laid her on the sofa she murmured, 'I never thought to see visions.' Her hands were waxen against the purple colours of her dress.

'I'll make you a cup of tea as soon as I've carried you back.' He was afraid that she might faint, have some sort of seizure, and he had no idea how to manage. He had been a fool to comply with her wishes. 'Or should I fetch you one now?'

'No. Tea's no answer.' Struggling, she raised her shoulders, contrived to prop herself on an elbow. 'He said I'd seen the last of him. At the end of it all he said that. "So be it," he said, quiet through the door, "I'll not bother you again." '

The skin on her face was like grey dust. 'It was Black Monday, as we call it, the evening of the day they closed the dam; and it was blacker before the night was out. He'd started with shouting: "You know it had to be done. I didn't want Linden to go, you know that. You know I would have prevented it if I could." He was yelling like a man gone mad. "So don't accuse me of being satisfied. I know the cost. As you once sneered, it's more than the price of cement. I know what it's costing you all to lose Linden. When I came to this job I didn't anticipate it was to build a watery grave." '

Lightning flamed over the pictures round her, bleaching their colours to spectral white. 'He was banging on the door, his knuckles like hammers, and between whiles he told me, "I'm going to the village. It'll have disappeared by the end of the month. And I'm asking you to come with me, Agnes. Come and stand with me. Say with me: It couldn't be stopped. Come and say with me: The reasons were too strong for us both." He whispered that, the begging, over and over again, sensing I was on the other side of the door. I didn't shift but I knew he would go for the knob. And for the first time in my life I turned the key in the lock. I watched the knob go round and I heard the breath leave him like bellows squashed flat.

'Tucked away in a corner of my mind was respect for that man, and he had a part of my heart. It wasn't right he came to the end he did.'

Fergal was kneeling by her side, straining to hear her. The thunder buffeted the house; any moment he thought it would blast open the room. 'Tell me.'

Her eyes did not move from the skylight behind him.

'He walked back to Linden. Walter Ibbotson was there taking a last look at his garden and gave him a good night. He spoke not a word but lifted up an iron bar that had been left in Edward's smithy and he carried it off. After he was done, Walter followed him the way he had taken and found him on Donkey Lane bridge. The pillars were built of stone but the top was laid with planks and he was going at them with the bar, heaving them up – they were heavy as railway sleepers – and casting them into the river. "Now then," Walter shouted, "steady does it," thinking him drunk. "You stop that and go home quietly." But he took no notice. Walter couldn't risk leaping over the gap, by the time he got there six planks had gone, yet he couldn't leave the man gabbling and sobbing to himself, despite who he was. So he shouted again, "You stop that. It's a senseless antic. And it's not safe." Because the river was flowing fast and I've told you there are treacherous currents. "Safe?" he shrieked back. "Nothing's safe with me about, is it? I'm one of those that are putting Linden under water, aren't I? I'm one of the demolition squad." Walter told him, "That's right, only nobody'll be walking over that bridge by the month end, so it's a waste of labour knocking it down." "I've finished with reason," he yelled, still forcing up the planks like a lunatic. "I've had enough of reasoning with you all. It did no good." He straightened up, raised his head from his task, and Walter saw that it wasn't sweat that was running down his face. Then he ordered, "Now let me be." So Walter left him.

'The next morning there was one plank left. The bolts

in it were bent, showing how the wood had been prised up a few inches. Wedged underneath it was the iron bar.'

Fergal imagined the muscles fighting the resistance of the bolts, the sudden slight give causing the legs to stagger, to throw the body off balance, and then the arc of its fall. 'So it was an accident,' he whispered.

'That was the coroner's verdict.'

But he knew it was not hers. Still she could not look at him. 'I locked the door against him. I heard him, his lips on the wood, say to me, "Goodbye, Agnes." He had to wait till the tears had ebbed down his throat before he could finish. "I shan't bother you again." '

She halted. There was hardly a pause now between the thunder and lightning. 'He was wrong when he said that. He's haunted me for the last eighteen years.' Her eyes dropped from the skylight and she peered into corners. Alarmed, Fergal leaned over her, tried to ease her onto the cushion but she resisted.

'I've never declared against ghosts, Fergal. They travel with us, wraiths in the mind, not creatures to see and touch.' The words tumbled out; now each cheek was patched with red.

He thought: Mother was right; Mrs Helliwell does seem to be heading for a fever. 'I have to get you to bed.'

Agnes ignored him. 'My ghosts have never come to me, not come like themselves. They have never laid down beside me or walked by my side. But this one has come. Today, he's come back.'

He had to humour her so he asked, 'Where?'

'In the only place he thinks is free to him. He doesn't

know that today the door is unlocked.'

'I see.' He stood up to suggest that he was ready to carry her down.

'Don't you judge that I'm sick. I've seen him, the true shape of him as he lived and breathed, out there on Donkey Lane bridge.'

'Perhaps it was a trick of the lightning.'

'Don't make me out daft.'

'It's a long way. Perhaps it's the angle; you've mistaken one of the pillars of the bridge.'

'The years haven't put paid to my eyes.' She forced her legs off the sofa and sat on its edge. Facing him, she challenged, 'Why don't you take a look for yourself?'

'I don't see what good that'll do. He's your ghost, not mine.' The words rippled cold over his skin.

'You fetch those binoculars that came from your grandfather. They'll not lie. They'll show the man as he was, right to the very hat.'

Hat. Who had mentioned one? His mother had said: 'There's a danger of sunstroke. You should wear a hat.' No; that wasn't it. Then he recalled another voice: 'I've got one or two of his things – his drawings, his favourite hat.'

Fergal had no memory of rushing into his bedroom, of rummaging through the drawers, suitcase, clothes, but when he stood on the chair, his head pushing out of the skylight, he had the binoculars to his eyes. Not stopping to focus, finding only an imprecise sheen of water and a blurred stump, he spun the knurled wheel. And it seemed as if a post, a spire, was rising out of the reservoir and clasped to its tapering sides was a man who held a flute to his lips. Then as Fergal turned the wheel, the crinkling water was exactly delineated and the spire was condensed into the pier of a bridge. On top of it, and far from the reservoir's edge, was the hump of a figure. Through the glasses the clothing shone wet; he could see the fingers splayed across the masonry and the legs looped round. A hand's breadth beneath them, between the two piers and running under the surface of the reservoir, was the river.

He knew that he was looking at Alex but alarm would not let him accept until he had seen her face. It was hidden under the wide brim of a hat, the kind that is waterproof, made of waxed fabric. And in the second of watching, he saw her head jerk up, surprised by a drop of rain. Simultaneously some hit the skylight, then great gouts splattered on the glass.

'It's her!' he shouted.

'Her?'

'Alex Bennet.'

She did not argue. 'So he's spared me.' Her mouth trembled with gratitude and relief. But that was fleeting. 'How did she get there? You must go to her.'

'I'm going.' He laid the binoculars on the escritoire. They were not needed.

Agitated, Agnes tried to rise as if she would accompany him. 'You told me last night she was set on getting to the bridge and I paid no attention, put myself first. As I did with her father.'

'Hang on to my neck and I'll carry you down.'

'No, I'll not delay you. If she slips, she'll be swept into

183

the river current. It must not claim another. No harm must come to that girl, the daughter of Matthew Bennet.' It was the first time she had spoken his name.

'I can reach her in fifteen minutes,' he said at the door. Could he? Nearer twenty, flat out.

'Yes. You fetch her, bring her here. I said I'd never forget. Or forgive them, Fergal, but I've learnt it's forgiveness I need for myself.'

Downstairs as he ran along the passage Fergal glanced into Agnes's room. His father's mobile phone lay on the bedside table. Grabbing it, he leaped back up the stairs, dumped it on the sofa, heard thanks, saw the rain shooting through the skylight on the gusts of storm wind. In the kitchen he told Gyp, whimpering under the table, 'Go find your mistress,' and pushed her towards the stairs.

Then he went into the dairy and collected the waders and the rope.

Nineteen

When he stepped out of the door, Fergal passed into a turbulent world. It was as if the old one of heat and drought, of still air and parched land must be violently destroyed before a new order could take its place. Swilling down the roof, the rain spilled over the gutters; its sharp points pricked his scalp as he hung the rope round his neck and tucked the waders under his arm. His trainers splashed through rivulets that were rapidly spreading and he heard the sound of their passage, deep throated, echoing in the drains. The wind tugged the stable door open, swung it on grinding hinges, and lightning showed him the aerial on a chimney bend and twist in the snatch of a gust.

The wood, too, was buffeted. Though dark as night under the shutter of the storm it was shot with brilliance when lightning blazed through the trees. The wind, finding the strips of paths, scratched up and scattered the pine cones, banged against shrubs and at times its skirl muffled the thunder's noise. The rain did not reach the ground here. Despite its force it could not penetrate the dense branches until they were sodden and leaked with its weight. So for the first stretch of Fergal's journey the going was easy. Sheltered against the worst of the storm's fury he ran the whole length of the wood and jumped without effort over obstacles and troughs.

But reaching Linden he had no protection. As it swept down the funnel of Crashing Beck the wind punched out his breath and the rain tore at him, lashing his skin. Beyond the church and nearer the reservoir it poured down the slopes, scraped off the brittle dust, pebbles and weeds. These slid under his feet, the grip of his trainers useless, until he reached the firmer surface of Donkey Lane. It curved into the water towards the stone pillar where Alex crouched.

Not for one moment since he started from the farmhouse had his thoughts left her. He had prayed: 'Don't leave go of the pillar, Alex. Don't let yourself slide off.' Now his muscles loosened with relief that she was still there. But he thought: How much longer can she hold on? He could feel the rain streaming off her head and striking her shoulders; he flinched as her denims stuck cold to her legs; and he sensed that the shirt which clung to her body was greasy with the sweat of fear. As was his.

Coming to the water's edge, swaying as his trainers sank into the swelling mud, he shouted, 'Alex!'

She waved quickly then hunched down again.

'I've got a rope.' Thunder blasted away his words. He pointed to the coil round his neck.

All he heard was: 'No' and 'far,' but that was enough.

He held up the waders and waggled them.

She shook her head and the wind brought him: 'No . . . pole . . . deep.'

Did that mean she had taken a sounding? 'Where's the pole?' He had never shouted so loudly. It peeled his throat. She removed a hand from the pillar; a finger pointed downwards.

'Don't let go!' This time he was shrieking. 'NOD IF I'M RIGHT. Did you lose it in the water?' Then he swore at himself; the pole was irrelevant.

Her nod went on a long time and he thought: She could be suffering from exposure. How long does it take?

'Did you get there from the other side? NOD OR SHAKE YOUR HEAD.'

Her lips moved but the words were splintered by the storm.

'NOD OR SHAKE YOUR HEAD.'

Both her hands came up, making a trumpet at her mouth. 'Not dumb,' he heard. 'Other side . . . nearer.' So she had approached from the opposite bank.

'Understood!' he bellowed and pointed up river.

Then, horrified, he saw a hand leave the pillar again and creep up to her face. Over the water and through the clap of the wind came a thin wail: 'Fergal . . . dizzy . . . scared.'

It sounded in his ears as he tramped back to Linden, as he passed the church. He listened to it as he folded the waders through the rope to free his hands for the climb up the mill, and its echo had not ceased when he entered Crashing Beck Lane. There he was checked briefly by a bag that blew against him. It contained litter and he imagined Alex collecting it as she had considered, performing a service to the dead village under the lightning's flares. The picture in his mind changed and became a figure perched in an expanse of water and again he heard the lonely, piping cry. Its rhythm accelerated and became more urgent, matching the pulse of his heart.

At the end of the lane no cars were parked where they had been on the day he returned from Niddford. No sightseers ventured out in this storm. Nor were there any vehicles using the road. Fergal raced down it, crossed the bridge, jumped a wall and followed the river's course. Once its banks had been thickly wooded, now they were stubbled with black polished stumps. Great roots stretched out, anchors for phantom trees, but today they were hooks that tripped his feet. At a sudden descent he skidded over the rain-sluiced ground among streams of silt and he saw that he was beside the falls of the river. They no longer dropped languidly over their rocky ledges but tumbled and frothed.

Alex was right. On this side of the reservoir the stretch of water in front of the bridge was narrower but it was still very broad. The wind swung round, bearing her voice clearly: 'Keep to the lane, but watch out.'

He levered off his sodden trainers and struggled with the waders. Forcing them against the resistance of his dripping denims and feet, he caught sight of his watch. The second hand clicked. He must reach her before . . .

At last he was in the water, splashing along the shelf of Donkey Lane. Swayed by his movements it shone pale under him until, further out, its reflection was dashed by the wind. This scooped up the water into myriad peaks of foam. But the lane remained firm and led him safely towards Alex until she called out: 'That's where I slipped.'

The water was above his knees; soon it would be over the waders. Through the wind and the rain that beat at his face, he shouted, 'How did you get there?'

'Don't know. Thrashed about. Swam. Grabbed. There's a plank.'

The one her father could not prise up. Fergal shuddered. Behind her, whipped by the wind, the river rushed into the reservoir; below her its course was invisible, pinned between steep banks; round her the reservoir had depths that could not be measured. No longer stagnant, slapped into life by the storm, it was mysterious, a place of dread. Fergal's mind was jabbed by apprehension but it did not reach his legs. Yelling to her, 'Stay still!' he lunged forward, saw her mouth open. Then the water was gushing up his chest, his feet were sliding and he was floundering, fighting against the drag of the waders, desperate to keep his head out of the water and not knowing whose scream it was that clashed in his ears.

When he had at last found the lane and ploughed back, he snarled to himself: 'You nutter. Just going for it, not working anything out.' He threw aside the waders and yanked off his denims, repeating, 'Didn't work anything out. Rushed into it. Just like before.'

However, today the situation was different, and he had brought a rope. Doubling one end of it over, he tied a large knot and with the coil over his left arm waded back. When the water came to his waist he stopped.

'If you can catch this,' he shouted, 'I'll keep it taut

while I pull you out.' Holding the rope in his left hand he grasped the knotted end some yards down its length. As he swung it over his head, he shook out the coil. Released, it arched, curved downwards, was taken by the wind. He watched it fall yards away from the pillar. Even if the wind had dropped for a second and the rope had been long enough, Alex could not have made a grab for it without risking her balance. He had forgotten his anxiety about that. As he had ignored the obvious fact that the rope was too short.

Drawing it in, he told himself savagely, 'And you know why you threw it. Come on, own up! You were hoping that all you'd have to do was hold on to the bleeding thing and pull.'

He could see that Alex's legs were no longer gripped round the stones and her body sagged. Bruised by the storm, she must be exhausted, freezing. Already his own skin was frosted with pimples and the water he stood in felt like liquid ice.

But that was bearable. It was the knowledge of what he must do that was congealing his blood.

He must do it. Now. He must not let himself think.

Fergal hung the rope round his neck and fastened it to his waist. Then he dipped into the water, his arms sliced and his feet churned up spray.

It seemed minutes before he reached her.

Less than two months earlier he would have been exhilarated by the response of his muscles and by the rhythm of the strokes. When he was fully submerged, the cold would pass and he would be in harmony with the water, meeting it strength for strength. Diving under, he would feel it sift his hair and he would watch his hands waft, slow and graceful as the gossamer fins of a fish. But all that was before an evening in June, before he had sat on the grass counting the seconds, before he had let out a great shriek and gone slithering down the bank.

And today once again he was thrusting through water; it had been feeble, ghostly, but now it was reborn. He could not control his breathing; he imagined he would sink. He had to tell himself that this reservoir did not hide something struggling, snared. Yet as his face skimmed the surface, memory would not let him open his eyes.

His hands scratched against stone, touched fabric. He lifted his head and found Alex above him. She said, her voice creaking, 'Glad . . . you've come.'

'Soon have you out.'

Close to her, he could see that her skin was shadowed with blue and her whole body was shaking. His own was weak, finished. It was as if he had swum miles.

'Don't . . . didn't . . .' The words were slurred. 'Didn't like . . . thunder. Glad's gone.'

He had not noticed. Nor that the lightning no longer jagged across the sky. But the rain still pounded. It glossed her shirt and denims like oil. Her hat dripped and flapped against her face while the wind wrenched at the strings securing it under her chin.

'I like the hat,' he told her. Her smile was slow to come.

The water swished round his neck. He stretched down but his toes could not find the bottom. Nearly five metres away was the pillar that stood on the opposite bank of the river. Agitated by waves, two shadows stretched towards it; they were the timbers that had carried the planks of the bridge. Across them and close to Alex's pillar, was the remaining plank. Fergal reached to it, carefully folding up his legs to avoid the river's current. As he hauled himself on to the wood, a bolt scraped his palm; he saw the blood toss in the water like a delicate plume.

'Fergal, can't . . .' A blast of wind took her next words. He saw an arm lift and quiver.

'No need to talk. Just keep holding on to that stone.'

'But . . . can't understand . . . why Dad . . . this bridge . . . only one . . .'

'One plank?'

'Yes.'

'Leave that till later.' He was unwinding the rope. Soaked through, it was heavy and cumbersome.

'Sat . . . here . . . puzzling . . . was a trap?'

'How?'

'Loosening the planks . . . taking some up . . . a trick . . . they did . . . Dad fell through?'

'No, they didn't do that.' He was trying to make a loop; his fingers were too cold.

'You know?'

'Alex, not now.'

'Please, Fergal. Please. I got here . . . but still don't . . . how Dad . . . why like this . . . a bridge . . . but only one plank.'

'Your father tore the others up. Mrs Helliwell told me.'

'No!'

'It's true. They didn't do it, Alex.'

'If not . . . what?'

'It was an accident. Mrs Helliwell wants to be the one to explain. You'll let her?'

She did not answer him; her head was bowed, her eyes on the water. It whirled under her, struck the pillar and collared it with foam. Then, draining off, it was bounced into points by the rain.

'Rotten place to die,' she murmured.

He gripped her wrist. 'Alex.'

She did not look up, swaying, mesmerised.

'Alex, listen.' He had put an arm round her shoulder. 'I have to get this loop on you.'

It was across her thighs and she looked at it in wonder.

'I want you to have a rope. It'll be safer. Support you. You can hold it, keep afloat, while I pull you in.'

That was the theory.

'So we have to get your arms through.'

Slowly her fingers crawled towards the loop. 'Thought I might . . . pass out,' she whispered.

'Yes.'

'Shouldn't have risked . . . Shouldn't have made you . . .'

'That's no matter now.' With his free hand he lifted the loop and she tried to raise an arm but it fell against her chest. The movement disturbed her balance; to steady her Fergal took his hand from the loop and in that snippet of time it reared, was hooked by the wind and slithered away. Behind it, the rope uncoiled, snaked into the water. They watched it drift and sink.

'Sorry.' Her face creased. 'My fault.'

'No. It was a stupid idea.'

It was stupid because she would never have been able to hold it and keep her head up, yet he had persuaded himself that it was possible.

'I brought it because . . .' He felt the panic rise from his stomach, stick in his chest. The rain was sheet steel. He could not see the width of the water, where its edge was.

He managed to say to her, 'Trying to fasten the rope on you was the same as me slinging it. Though it was too short. Because I was telling myself it would do the work, save you. Without having me. It can't, but I had to believe you'd be all right if you had the rope.' He could not make the words have his meaning. 'I had to keep thinking: She can depend on the rope. Better than trying to depend on me.' The wind struck his mouth, beating away the air. He thought he would choke. 'I can't trust myself.'

She looked at him and he knew that, despite her exhaustion, she understood. 'You got here. Swam. Made a crack in the block.'

'Perhaps.'

Her mouth was skewed because of the numbness. 'I think perhaps I have, too.'

For a moment they stayed there, oblivious of the cold, of rain and wind, his arm round her and she heavy against him. Then her shaking began again.

He said to her, 'You can't leave your hat on. It'll float off.'

'Mustn't lose. Hold.' But as she fumbled with the strings, she admitted, 'Hands no good. Teeth?'

So he drew off the hat, squeezed out a section of the brim and pushed it into her mouth; then he slid into the water.

He tried not to think about what he was doing. When he put a hand on her waist and instructed, 'Lean back and I'll catch you,' he contrived to ignore the pain in his chest. But as she entered the water and his hands clasped her head, his mind lurched. For he felt the current of the river rush under the plank and tug at his legs.

Twenty

The diminished strength of the river was restored by the wind and the rain; under the reservoir the banks nipped the flow into a spate that was impossible to resist. Fergal's first thought was: Keep clear of the pillar, but he avoided it by luck, not skill. The current crashed into the masonry, leaped up it in a sickle of spray, fell back, then swung and twirled them in its sucking rings. Fergal had to fight to keep afloat. He could do nothing more. He caught a glimpse of the two stubs of pillars but he could not make for the edge of the water; he had no idea where that was, and the river commanded. The next time he saw the pillars they were far away which meant he was approaching the centre of the reservoir. He assumed that the current would be weaker there.

He said to himself: I ought to turn, strike out, the bank must be somewhere. For, if he could not make his legs answer his brain, he might take Alex as far as the dam and he imagined them both smashing into it, stunned, drifting then sinking, their bodies spread-eagled against the base of its wall. But it was not sensible to change course, or try to, he persuaded himself, until he knew their direction. Soon he promised he would make the effort to find out.

He had packed in a lot since breakfast. He was starving; no wonder his muscles were nothing but mush. His legs were weighted with cold and that was bad for you, paralysing. He wondered what state Alex was in. At least, since he was moving his legs, a bit, his blood should be circulating. Whereas she was inert, dragging at his arms. He couldn't see the hat but it might be hidden by her head. Unless she was finished, she wouldn't let go of it. You would expect to see it bobbing about. If it wasn't there, it meant that . . .

Between his hands, her head did not stir; he could feel the bumps of her skull. Was he pulling a corpse? Give over, he ordered himself. That's enough of that.

The rain rapped his face but squinting through it he looked at the sky. From this position it did not seem as dark as when he had left the farm. What time was that? Turning his head slightly, he could see a line on the horizon, black, a black strip. A long beam of light was skimming the top of it. For a moment Fergal puzzled, then he recognised the dam and a speeding vehicle. He watched it climb the hill and turn, its light flashing through the trees, and immediately he had his bearings. Yesterday he had cycled along that road on his way to the field cemetery. So on his right was the side of the reservoir where he and Alex had started out.

Gripping her tightly, he kicked with his right foot; she tilted as he swung her round, her head struck his chest and he was swamped with water. It poured into his mouth, spouted up his nose, then he went under.

The water was dark but it soon paled to twilight,

subdued and clear. To his surprise, his eyes were not stung by sand rising in flurries and there was no sign of the wire that had snared Bailey in its barbs. That day, Bailey had been lifted away, but he had left an echo:

'The incident in the river is history now.'

Fergal's own voice answered: *'I've got a block. Something went wrong.'*

But Alex's voice insisted: *'You've swum here, made a crack in that block.'*

And his father murmured: *'Other people might let you off the hook but it's hard learning to forgive yourself.'*

While all the time above Fergal's head was a figure framed by glass and silhouetted against shafts of light. This figure swayed, the hair fanned, he saw that it was Alex; and, as his lungs bulged, threatened to rupture, he understood that throughout those crammed seconds he had not let her sink. He had supported her on the water's surface, his arms straight and his hands firm round her head.

He slid upwards gently, kept her steady while he spluttered and belched. Then he measured the distance from the bank, his feet drove at the water and he felt it buckle and give.

Now the strokes of his legs were smooth and confident. He knew that he would get Alex out. He accepted the water and the cold; he was not troubled by fatigue. Nor did memories hamper him with fear or remorse. Because he had done it. Today he had not allowed the water to defeat him, he had not panicked when faced with someone helpless, needing his ingenuity and strength. Even when he was swept under. He had proved to himself that he could hold out however frightened he was. That made the other time, the time with Bailey, more bearable. So Fergal pulled Alex to the side of the reservoir and was serene with himself, glad.

His heels skidded on ground; it was soft. His shoulders were out of the water and there were people round him. He tried to raise himself but he could not do it without relinquishing his clasp on Alex's head. Someone took her weight. 'You can let go of her now, Fergal,' a voice instructed.

Another one said, 'I'll see to him.'

Peering, his eyes hazed with water, Fergal could make out Wellington boots. They were filthy with mud. A waterproof cape glistened.

Desmond Singleton put his hands under Fergal's armpits and lifted him up. 'Come on now,' he encouraged and, supporting him, he guided Fergal a little way up the bank.

It seemed to have stopped raining and the wind had reduced to a slicing draught, but its cold still clutched. His jaws were set solid. Staggering, he gestured to three figures who were holding a bundle in the sling of a rug.

'The lass will be fine,' Desmond interpreted his question. 'Hang on to my shoulders while I pummel you dry. But I have to admit she gave us a turn. I had a peek through those binoculars of yours. I wasn't sorry I wasn't perched up where she was.'

He pointed again. 'Sure?'

'Don't you worry yourself. She's got Walter and

Gilbert. The other's the doctor. He looks cheerful enough.'

'Soaked. Alex. For ages.'

'She's a strong one, managed a word or two once she'd given up that hat. We couldn't make out what it was wagging about. Can you hold this rug round you while I dry your back? I must say, Fergal, there's not a lot you can be taught about swimming. Your father said she was in good hands.'

'Dad?'

'He gave Mrs Helliwell a ring to check how she fared, the weather being what it was. Do you think you could swing your arms, whip up a bit of heat? I've a couple of Martin Helliwell's jerseys under this cape.

'It was a good job your father left that telephone of his, Mrs Helliwell got us all hopping. Now he's gone with Toby Wheatley, see if they can fetch the truck closer, get that young woman up to the farm.'

'I want to see her.'

'Pull these trousers on first, don't want you charged with indecent exposure.'

Alex was lying on a tarpaulin swaddled in blankets. Her skin was pinched, bluish but she was not shaking. Walter Ibbotson was filling a hot water bottle from a flask while Gilbert Beardsall supported her head and held a cup to her lips. He told Fergal, 'Your mother's warming a bed for her and she's put soup in that thermos. Get it down you.'

Alex slid her mouth from the cup. 'Fergal,' she said, 'thanks.'

'No.' With the others there, he could not remind her: If it hadn't been for you I might never have dared. All he could attempt was: 'Pulling you, I thought you might be . . . because the water was arctic.'

'Worse. But . . . not . . . worried.' Her eyes did not leave his face. 'Did it. I was . . . satisfied.'

She had sat on the bridge, had seen where her father had fallen. Fergal nodded, then frowned as coughing heaved through her.

When it was finished, she whispered, 'Don't look . . . so anxious. Won't be long before . . . recovered. Have it . . . on . . . good authority.' A smile was a possibility.

'That's so,' the doctor agreed, keen to identify the authority. 'But if she'd been out another half hour, it would have been a different story. You did splendidly. It was a piece of luck, wasn't it, that you happened to be walking by.'

'Yes. It was lucky. Just the right time.'

Amused, the three Linden men looked at Fergal. They said nothing but their faces glinted with the knowledge that he and they shared.

Then headlights beamed and the truck began to crawl down the slope that had once led to a bridge over a river, along a track called Donkey Lane.